Srishti Khanna is a Punjabi middle-class lass with mentors in the avatar of social gods, and very much a part of every colourful character described in the book. Srishti grew up in this city but also lived in other cities in India, which helped her draw a few comparisons and define Dilliwalas as abnormally normal. A lady of remarkable achievements, Srishti has earned her stripes running bars and restaurants, and getting to know everyone worth knowing in this city, post a few...shhhhhhh!

AF673126

DilliLeaks

Srishti Khanna

Foreword

Suhel Seth

OM

Om Books International

First published in 2015 by

OM
Om Books International

Corporate & Editorial Office
A-12, Sector 64, Noida 201 301
Uttar Pradesh, India
Phone: +91 120 477 4100
Email: editorial@ombooks.com
Website: www.ombooksinternational.com

Sales Office
107, Ansari Road, Darya Ganj,
New Delhi 110 002, India
Phone: +91 11 2326 3363, 2326 5303, 4000 9000
Fax: +91 11 2327 8091
Email: sales@ombooks.com
Website: www.ombooks.com

Text copyright © Srishti Khanna
Foreword copyright © Suhel Seth

ALL RIGHTS RESERVED. No part of this book may be reproduced or transmitted in any form by any means, electronic or mechanical, including photocopying and recording, or by any information storage and retrieval system, except as may be expressly permitted in writing by the publisher.

ISBN: 978-93-83202-32-4

Printed in India

10 9 8 7 6 5 4 3 2 1

Contents

For Subhash Khanna, my father
(1946-2013)

Acknowledgements

I thank...

Ma and Pa for paying up my school fees regularly despite my report cards, for trusting me to make the right and wrong choices by myself, for not getting me checked for a hole in my head, and for resisting the occasional temptation of taking me to an asylum;

All the colourful personalities who inspired this book;

All those who, in plainspeak, polished off midnight bottles with me before coming up with many crazy ideas;

All the gossip sessions without which this book would never have happened;

My friends (yes, in alphabetical order; who wants a bloodbath) Akhil Mittal, Anish Chanana, Arshad Siddique, Gaurav Chhabra, Meenakshi Iyer, Meghna Syal Chadha, Minakshi Singh, Munny Sethi, Pavan Jhamnani, Payal Suri, Rajat Sanghi, Rashmi Chhabra, Reena Chadha, Suparna Krishna, for being a part of my life and the book;

Suhel Seth for writing the Foreword in the same vein as he speaks on governance in India;

Ajay Mago and Dipa Chaudhuri for insisting I get beyond just drunken banter, and for making sure, *without any indulgence,* that I reached the finishing line. Thank you for not giving up on me and for making me feel like a genius, even if I am the only one who thinks so.

And finally, ladies and gentlemen, thank you in advance for not ostracising me.

Foreword

Srishti Khanna provides an insider's guide into the Dilli as we know it but try and shun most of the time. It is the arrogance of the old that prevents us from accepting the harsh reality that Delhi is no longer Delhi. It is, in fact, Dilli. It is this Dilli that is both the great leveller and the terrible unifier. Where Lajpat Nagar and Lutyen's meet but in not so palatable environs. This is no longer the city of the powerful and the rich. It is also the city that has as its citizens, those who really don't care about power as long as there is money going with it. This is the Dilli where water is scarce and yet pool parties make it to Page 3. This is also the city where people are known by what they wear on their bodies rather than what they are made up of within. Money is the currency of knowledge and not pure intellect. In many ways, Dilli is bought and sold every day. For some, with money and for others, with influence. And they all wield it in some form or the other. The politician does so through power till he or she loses an election; the industrialist does so through money until, of course, he is summarily confined to Tihar Jail. But each of the players, captured on this wonderful landscape by Srishti Khanna, tell a story like it has never been told before.

Like most cities in the world, Dilli too has its own lexicon: one which is stated and the other that is unstated. The red beacon atop an ugly SUV says a lot about where you come from and where you are headed. As does the farmhouse that you stay in which has all the flora and fauna but no heart. But then these are the choices that an expansive and all-embracing Dilli allows you to make.

The wonderful thing about this book is it does not judge. Which is such a relief because Dilli judges its people every day and then changes the statutes of such judgement when convenient. I have seen people being shunned as soon as they are in trouble but then welcomed with fake affection as soon as they are able to send out yet another invitation.

To many, this will be a book about Dilli. But to others it will also be a telling study of who we are and what we have become. It is not just a anthropological study of the people that make up Dilli today but is also a guide to the future that we are carving for the denizens who will inhabit Dilli. This is where the book triumphs. It takes you on a self-discovery within the context of how cities shape human behaviour and vice versa. It is sans jargon but with a great deal of soul: ironic because that is what is missing in most of the Dilli that is talked about in the book.

In many ways, Julian Assange would approve of the title of this book. And we, in turn, would be relieved that Srishti will not be committed to an Ecuadorian Embassy for the rest of her life but instead continue to probe and pry in order to build a more robust case for a city that has now become the lingua franca for a nation that is at an inflection point.

Suhel Seth

Ode to Dilli

For every smile I faked,
At all their jokes half-baked,

At all the bar entrances I graced,
For all those slurs I braced,

When slight came my way,
I fought to hold my sway.

Each smirk of mine I hid,
And did as I was bid,

I gulped a high tear tide,
Soothing some clunk's bruised pride,

With every tip I made,
For their whims and fancies I paid.

More the fool I just became,
Blissfully unaware of their game,

Till finally I decided to 'mend,'
And dive in at their end,

Adopting the ways of sin,
I became a 'socially accepted' kin.

Today, perhaps I dare,
Much more than those I bare,

In Dilli, you can be king,
If you know the right notes to sing,

The city is with secrets ablaze,
As you crawl through its soulless maze,

While bravado helps me spill the beans,
A good Merlot is always the better means.

1

Chemical Composition of a Dilli-ite

Every substance is defined by its properties and the same holds true for the substance called Dilli-ite. Ergo, the breakdown—Dilli-ite = 15% Old Dilli + 30% Punjab + 10% Uttar Pradesh + 10% Haryana + 10% Bihar + 10% Bengal + 10% other cultures and nationalities + 5% riff-raff.

My own family is living proof of this mess. My mother's from a polite artistic family whose roots can be traced to Dilli of 1874. Right, we are talking about the Sepoy Mutiny/Indian Rebellion, give or take a couple of decades. Only the good Lord or a two-century old relative can explain how my mother's family merged with a family from Lahore where my dad-to-be would scramble onto rooftops and dine and hobnob with the entire neighbourhood without as much as an invite or a telephone.

Now that sure is an eccentric composition that goes into the formation of a Dilli-ite. Mind you, it's not the easiest load to carry around, being defined and fined for being a Dilli-ite. One must adopt the best and worst of every culture to be called a true Dilli-ite and not necessarily in that order.

So here's a beginner's survival kit for 21st-century Dilli:

Apply skin-thickeners in ample quantity. That helps ward off sarcasm, jibes and the Aedes mosquito.

At a party, carry your own bottle of malt; tip the bartender generously in front of everyone, even if you glug down Blender's Pride at home.

To win an argument, simply shriek.

To make yourself heard, just say with a mix of Sylvester Stallone and Clint Eastwood, assuming they speak Hindi, '*Tu janta nahi mera baap kaun hain.*' (You don't know who my father is.) Chances are nobody does, but hold your fort nonetheless.

Parade your top contacts, especially at Janpath Road and Raisina Hill, in case you get into serious trouble, and leave the rest to your personal security officers. If you don't, sometimes the bouncers in front of you come up with good solutions.

Strut into the stores that line the high street. Make sure news about your movements go viral, then secretly head out to the most down-market places, preferably in disguise, and bargain with street vendors.

Please tell everyone where you stay, especially if it is Golf Links, Jor Bagh, Aurangzeb Road, or a similar address in 'South' Dilli.

To be a fashion diva, cover or uncover yourself, depending on how you want to look at it, from head to toe in monogrammed Gucci, Louis Vuitton, Chanel, Dior, and Burberry. Just take care to not open your gab and give yourself away. Rome was not built in a day.

Don't believe that sod who tells you that you are too kind, friendly, fun loving, polite, happy, normal and sane to be a Dilli-ite; that you must be from Mumbai or Hyderabad or wherever he thinks the majority of good people live in this country.

Please do not confuse us with anyone else. Our foundation, our spirit is made of all that people complain about, but also love about us. And if there is a chink in our Arrogant Armani Armour, don't be startled. We'd rather you believe the worst about us and be pleasantly surprised by the best in us, and then be rudely shocked again. We prefer to be demonised or idolised than to be forgotten heroes. We Dilli-ites are not *insaan* (humans) we are insane! And proud to be so.

2

Dilli Boy

Seen one, seen them all. Who said anything of the sort?

They come in different colours, shapes, sizes, bank accounts, hairstyles, addresses, and are nicknamed after the cars they, or their chauffeurs drive (for them, extinct bird).

Do not get me wrong, I LOVE them! Gorgeous creatures, who, for want of a better word, are gullible. The gorgeous Dilli Boy believes a girl in hand is mandatory but a few in the bush are essential for his manliness. For a more detailed understanding of the subject, please see below:

Single Rich Boy

Top 3 lines (uttered seductively in the six different UN-approved languages):

1. Can I buy you a drink?
2. Can I buy you a car?
3. Can I buy you a house?

If you are an attractive unattached woman of any nationality, behold! You shall be swept off your feet, loved and pampered…for a month.

Sweethearts that they are, they might date a woman they are compatible with, fall in love with, a woman who intellectually stimulates them and sexually titillates them but will only pop the question to the girl that mother finds them.

How to detect a Single Rich Boy

Usually found driving top-end cars, with music blaring away, Cavalli clothing, Armani pointed shoes, stepping out only when the personal security officers (drivers are passé) open the car doors so he can float into a host of exclusive clubs and restaurants, followed by a trail of beautiful East European girls. A grand welcome awaits him not because he is a popular brat, but because of the American Express Centurion in his wallet and the generous tip that can buy the waiter his first Paul Smith muffler.

No need for prior reservation. That is only for earthworms like you and me. This boy is swept past the lines. In all fairness, I am with the club manager on this, because if you happen to break the unspoken rules of the brat's kingdom, the manager is bound to come down with a disabling migraine because of repeated chants of 'You don't know who I am?' or 'You don't know who I am with?'

Let's consider that you missed the grand entrance sans the caparisoned elephants and liveried footmen holding out velvet cushions, tell yourself you've missed nothing since the cobra shall raise its head again and again, till you wish you had spotted him earlier, and acquired immunity against him.

Like it or not, this boy grabs your attention with an array of alcohol shots that find their way into your hands through the good offices of emissaries such as friends and acquaintances. Then a Gout Du Diamant is uncorked and the bubbly drunk straight from the bottle. Are the French listening? The boy still feels unnoticed. Short of stripping, what next? He jumps on the table, the couch or on a woman.

One such dolt just has to jump on elevated surfaces. He's five feet two inches. I understand when he says he has spent five lakhs in a single night at a club I am managing, he has a right to be seen, any which way. No arguments.

In the end, this unique brand of subtlety will simply win you over!

I once went out on a date with one such Dilli Boy.

A bike ride on a Harley Davidson.

Destination: Prince Paan & Chaat Corner, Greater Kailash Part I.

It was 10 p.m. when I was greeted by an entourage outside my house—my date on his Harley Davidson, and three cars with personal security officers displaying a range of eye-wear chosen by the boss. Heart in mouth, I sat on the bike, and we zoomed across the city...at the speed of 30 km/h. Just as I was getting used to the potholes and the garbage truck ahead of us, a dust storm kicked in. My allergies surfaced. My running nose and watering eyes bled my mascara—the crowning moment of three precious hours spent earlier in the day perfecting my face.

Finally, the Prince Paan signage was in sight. For those who do not know Prince Paan, it's the nerve centre of the most popular market of the '90s, beautifully laid out around a colony park. A corner store open till 1 a.m., Prince Paan serves as an excuse to prolong a date, with delectable flavours wrapped in beetle leaf. Come to think of it, a mouth-refreshing experience is a perfect prelude to some extra-curricular activities.

With more than my hair in a mess, I got off the bike, my legs benumbed, ordered my *paan* and set out on a romantic walk around the block by moonlight with my date, only to be followed by seven uniformed security officers five steps behind us, carrying my handbag (part of their brief), and handing us Oudh-scented tissue to wipe the rich juicy spittle overflowing the corners of our mouth. Would love a job like that if it's well paid.

A ride back home was now the only route back to sanity and my own beloved planet. The magnificent display of power and wealth has till date ensured love from my neighbours (yes, they stayed awake till I was back). They were familiar with the concept of motorcades being escorted by motorcycles. A Harley escorted by cars was the cart before the ox. Ever since, they either doff their hat or step aside as a mark of respect as soon as they see me.

~

3

Single But Don't Mingle

Mingling with our Dilli Boy with rich genes begins with an uphill drive: private islands, jets, yachts, villas, Rolls-Royces, lavish spreads with credit cards and vacations to dreamlands visited only by Brangelina and their brood.

The lucky one could also be taken to fashion shows in Milan, gifted a new wardrobe of the latest season's collections, live in mansions with liveried staff, and receive a brand new Mercedes Benz on Janamashtami in celebration of the Divine Lover.

Her reputation may take a bit of a hit and she may be called 'arm-candy,' but we make small sacrifices right through life for the woods, don't we.

And if you think I am high on dope right now, the Dilli Boy shall openly boast of his miscellaneous expense accounts—the truth of his magnanimity recorded in his manual.

But watch out—getting emotionally attached to the dude is asking for trouble, Alprax, several boxes of tissue and a couple of 'I told you so' friends. Blind as he may be in his quest to be a cad, get your head out of the sand and hear him whisper (apologies Gibran), 'A little while, a moment of rest upon the wind, and another woman shall bare me.'

4

Wannabes

For the first time, my phone dictionary doesn't display anything insulting when I type in 'wannabe.' I guess I am finally getting good at the English language.

'Wannabe' means 'wanting to be someone you are not.' 'He/she is such a wannabe' is something I hear so often. And I have an uncontrollable urge to use the word for many people I come across each day.

If you are nice to people, since it's now an obsolete art, you are a wannabe; if you are not that nice, you are pretending to be a snob, hence you are a wannabe.

We are all social wannabes in this city, extremely territorial, over-protecting our hierarchy in the social circles to stay at the pinnacle. And of course, when another wants to topple us to that post, guess who is branded as a 'wannabe.'

Wannabe = Weed. It grows everywhere. Without the pleasure of anyone smoking it!

And no matter how hard you try to weed out wannabes, they spring right back, right in the front of the pretentious social garden. A genus classification may be of help.

Flowery

These look good from a distance, with all the makings of a charming socialite—fake bags, designer rip-offs and imaginary invites to the biggest dos in town (which they eventually gatecrash). Full of empty smiles and social chit-chat, they follow the protocol, so they call you up in the middle of the night, sweet talk you for half an hour after four months of silence, only to extract a social favour. Their mantra: cosy up to the socially powerful trees, grow under their shade, gain entry to greener pastures, then move on to even better fields. Remember, the idea is to overshadow the same tree in the end. This species is as prevalent as the common cold with a back-stabbing sneeze.

Prickly

These ones are either narcissists or suffer from verbal diarrhoea. They laugh at their own jokes, pretend everyone, who is someone, is their best friend. They can down gallons of booze and are bottomless pits to feed. Rude and obnoxious, they push people around and pretend they own the world (a way to ensure they aren't stopped at the entry of a fashion show they were never invited to).

I know a prickly weed who would invariably land up at my house, despite precautionary measures. Why, I had planned a girl's night out and invited some girls at home for pre-drinks. Excited, my status read 'Girls night out commencing from home.' It took all of five minutes thereafter for him to ring my doorbell, and polish off the last few drops of Macallan. Not knowing how to put a stop to his repeated uninvited intrusions—eight times in two months—I eventually changed my home.

Creeper

Forever wrapped around you, whether you like it or not, creepers that latch on are difficult to shake off. They monitor your every move and snake around you when you least expect them to. And don't flatter yourself if you have a creeper stalking you; it's only because there is no one else worth stalking, at least not till the bigger social catch comes along. So, try and enjoy the nagging till it lasts, or else buy them a quick drink to show your support and earn your right to avoid them for the rest of the evening.

Serpentine

Difficult to spot in a crowd, they live forever in denial of being wannabes. This is the most poisonous variety. They spread rumours about you, sabotage your businesses, steal your girlfriends, all with a poker face.

Now I know you too must be classifying people in different 'wannabe' categories but don't be surprised if someone else is slotting you as well. In the end, we all do *wannabe*...

5

Dilli Girl

Girl in her early twenties

Do they all look the same? *Yes.* Slim, petite, fair, long black hair (the straightening iron is a must on the vanity counter). And God help us if the bottle blond fad kicks in again with more LBDs than an entire army of Indian designers can create annually.

This young woman is always accompanied by a man entrusted with the responsibility of looking after her every need—drink, popcorn, even Kleenex to wipe the extra *kajal*. A happy submissive soul, she lets her man order her food. She has eyes for only one man unless someone better comes along the way. Fair enough. She is by far the most sought after woman in the world. The bigger her dream house where she can play 'raise the family,' higher the odds are in her favour, till intoxication overpowers her judgement—the Lord's way of balancing out the jungle law.

Every other woman in the room turns green with jealousy when she enters and every man hopes she may leave with him.

The stage is set, the game begins, the moves are made.

There are only two endings to this live show that takes place in front of a curious audience:

She gets married to her dream house.
Or
She remains single in her late twenties.

Single girl in her late twenties

Show some respect. She is still surviving the shit-creek of Dilli-Boy options. She has a cemented exterior, minus any cracks whatsoever, to efficiently keep the boil of emotions inside hidden from the public eye. She is an independent, tough woman who now comes and goes without holding on to a man's arm and walks without support.

She's happy.

She's bold.

She decides and she chooses.

She looks different. Not wilted. Fashion becomes a priority. Ambiguity develops into individuality.

Every fortnight, she yearns for her knight in shining armour, but now she wants a horse of her own and not a saddle that belongs to him. She wants to charge ahead, not follow.

She now goes from strength to strength for the next 10 years.

When the hunted becomes the hunter, a cougar is born. Or let's just say that's how I see it…

But, hold on. Beyond the constant gymming with the handsome sculpted personal trainer, is a threatened girl living in the constant fear of being ridiculed. She was raised with a simple plan: school, college, marriage, kids, diamonds and kitty parties. She is missing all the drama of a married couple's retreat.

Now, let's imagine her in an evening out. All her friends are either married or about to tie the knot. At the dining table are the 'made for each other' couples. And God help her if she hasn't managed to find herself a date.

Pleasantries exchanged, there's nothing more to talk about. The single woman is suddenly a new species of mammal with pink horns and green spots. Within half an hour, there are curious looks, suggestive remarks and then one idiot takes it upon himself or herself to start the conversation on the single woman's love life:

1. Who's the guy in your life?
2. Why don't you have a guy in your life?
3. Why haven't you found the right guy in your life?
4. What happened to the last guy in your life?
5. Shouldn't you have found the right guy and been married by now?
6. Do you plan to ever get married to a guy?
7. Are you scared of committing to a guy?
8. Do you like playing the field with more guys?

9. Do you realise your body clock is ticking away?
10. Are you gay?
11. Are you bisexual?

Some answers that I have copyrighted over the years are listed below:

1. Planning my future wedding gives my mother such joy that I hate to put an end to it.
2. My boyfriend is serving his jail sentence and anyway, his divorce hasn't come through yet.
3. I am still experimenting with my sexuality.
4. It is my dream to win the MISS India pageant someday.

If you don't set their concerns to rest ASAP, this single woman becomes a microbe under a microscope, scrutinised for the alien gene, lest it spreads. Worse still, her true friends treat her like a charity case that should be set up with *any* man who comes along *now*, for she can't find one herself. She must 'settle.' Now, that's the word with the promise of compromise, the word that may hold you back rather than let you rise up to what you believe you could possibly achieve.

Be that as it may, it'll still be about *the missing man.*

~

Two years back, (obviously I missed the last one) I went to a hotel bar with my dancing shoes on, to meet my classmates. It was a school reunion. Being overweight or a receding hairline was a minor matter. The fact that I was single took precedence over their rising cholesterol levels, shrinking arteries and slipped discs.

After an hour of hearing about their absent spouses, listening to stories of how they met their soulmates, their lovely wedding and their two little angels, I finally spotted two unmarried women. Yippie. Until, one of them brought me up-to-date about her planned wedding next year and the other one gloated about the alimony she had squeezed out of her ex-husband.

No, thank you. Such dinners and reunions are finally out of my planner.

6

A Night Out in the City

Live it up like it's the last night, especially those who have forgotten the exit route from *A Night at the Roxbury*.

There are impenetrable groups of Dilli Clubs—Gymkhana and Golf Club—to indicate pedigree. Either you are born into it or you could pull the right strings to extract an invitation. A price-sensitive option, it gives you the opportunity for daily social bonding and yet saves you enough for the new Chanel bag.

And now for an evening with generations of stuck-ups. This could be an epic movie set with the old world charm I hope this city never loses, where behind the iron gates, I can still see my grandfather in a beret, smoking his pipe while enjoying his jazz. Cut back to reality and you see a specimen in faded clothes holding a Marlboro (or an occasional cigar) while high-pitched greetings drown piped music in the background that no one cares about.

Today the 40-year-olds (yes, they are the young ones today) who have inherited this legacy, use it for an inexpensive gourmet evening with whiskeys imbibed from monogrammed glassware.

Yet, there is great respect for the elderly. Occasionally a wheelchair is parked outside the bar. Umbrella stands are full of walking sticks they use for a compulsory hourly walk not only to exercise the old bones but also to take phone calls outside the club premises, as is the rule. Even the servers who have become self-appointed dieticians suggest steamed and baked food options.

The live band has whittled down to a solo player belting out Frank Sinatra on a synthesizer that was invented by Bob Moog in 1963.

The appreciative guests dance, and some of them shake and shiver to an ambience of gaiety on the best night of the week. And some of the remaining are propped up by supplements prescribed by the physician on call every Thursday night—with compliments of the club management.

7

Dillwaley Dilliwaley

Despite excessive cholesterol, Dilliwales are very Dillwale. Their generosity, hospitality and the will to live life Dilli-Size are legendary. They also have a large stomach (oh those chicken *tikkas*!) and an unbeatable liver (Shots! Shots! Shots!). So allow me to take you on an experience of a weekend and I challenge you to find better entertainment in this country.

FRIDAY

8 p.m.: Dinner with family
10 p.m.: Pre-drinks at home or at a friend's house
11:30 p.m.: Appointing a leader to plan the evening
12 a.m.: First night club
1 a.m.: Dancing on the couch
1:30 a.m.: Seventh round of shots with minimal arm-twisting
2 a.m.: En-route second night club with women jumping out of car sun-roofs
2:30 a.m.: Dancing on tables and bar counters

3 a.m.: Champagnes pop
3:30 a.m.: DJ is replaced by us behind the console
4 a.m.: Fighting over paying the bill (Everyone wants to pay)
5 a.m.: Hotel Coffee Shop with *keema pav* or we head out to another venue for an after-party and a home-cooked meal (FYI, my favourite is a cheese omelette at 5:30 a.m. I can't remember the recipe sober.)

SATURDAY

2 p.m.: Hangover, a course of Aspirin and coffee
3 p.m.: Vague recollections of the previous night
6 p.m.: Previous night's mystery solved after numerous phone calls
7 p.m.: Evening party scheduled
10 p.m.: Encore

SUNDAY

1 p.m.: Frantic buzzing of mobile phones
2 p.m.: Pool party or Sunday brunch
3 p.m.: Sulking and nursing a hangover
5 p.m.: *Where's The Party Tonight?*

MONDAY MORNING

I Will Never Drink Again

~

If you are not from this part of the planet, doesn't matter. Your car keys will be taken, your mobile phones held at ransom and don't even bother looking for those handbags. Remember you are a captive till you start enjoying your captivity.

It's customary for Dilliwalas to feed 10,000 people over 10 days of festivities for a blissful life ahead for newly-weds, or so they claim. Family, family friends, friends and friends of friends are all invited. Invitations come from the bride and groom, their families, their friends, their neighbours, and other acquaintances.

My own sister's wedding was a carnival of 1400 people in which I didn't know 1300. (Thank god for alcohol.)

Drink, dance, sing, sin, eat and enjoy if you want to be a part of the immediate family's dining table.

The occasions are innumerable and always special:

1. Dad's birthday in a posh hotel where music blares on the terrace till 7 a.m. and Blue Label flows.
2. Lakhs paid for the sister's engagement to hire a renowned singer only to have the stage eventually taken over by us.
3. Girlfriend's belated birthday after a month with a thousand people in attendance, and never-ending flow of food and spirits.

A Dilliwala opens his heart along with his house and his wallet. A few drinks down though, he might open a bit more.

8

Love is in the Air

A friend's engagement was being planned when her parents decided they wanted the blessings of Gurudwara Sri Hemkunt Sahib in the Himalayas. It's located in the state of Uttarakhand bordering Tibet and Nepal, and is accessible only between the months of June and October.

Says who?

We went in February as that was the auspicious month for the engagement. This *we* comprised 180 guests.

As our cars pulled up in front of the airport, out stepped a Punjabi army dripping with diamonds, in sarees and *lehengas* (Indian flared skirt). Other travellers watched an in-house wedding procession, with merry-makers sipping pre-mixed drinks, giggling and dancing all the way to the aircraft.

As we boarded the chartered Airbus A320, found our seats and followed the safety instructions to buckle our seat belts, the *dholwala* (percussionist) walked in. Punjabi *boliyan* (lyrics) took off at the same time as the aircraft. And we danced in the plane on economy class seats, literally painting the skies blue while the pilot perfected his prayers at record speed.

Soon we could see the snow-capped peaks of the Sapt Shring. Rings were exchanged while the aircraft hovered directly over Hemkunt Sahib. Then we returned to Dilli.

And for those of you who believe I have had a drink too many, this exorbitant Dilliwala exists, and has offered to do action replay for my wedding. Except, the groom is still in the making.

9

ACCENTuate Yourself

A good grasp of Hindi as a language is a sin and should be kept under wraps. It sounds rowdy, uncouth and makes your companions shifty not only about your conversation style and drift, but about knowing someone like you. Your education is worth it only if it includes international languages even if you know only three cool phrases in each.

If you must, use Hindi to communicate with domestic help at a luncheon or with a driver at the porch; spice it up with an unheard of diction to prove the language taught to you for 14 years is actually alien to you.

You are, however, allowed to use it in bits and pieces. Profanity is cool. Slangs are best when quoted from a hit Bollywood song. It's now a street language and the fact that it has twice the amount of alphabets English has, and is just a few centuries older, still doesn't prove its worth.

The Re-Pats (Indians who relocate in India) make it a must to use English as a heavily accented language. It's so much in vogue that even if your passport has a single-entry visa to a country of whites, you would have earned your right to roll your tongue. A trip to Sri Lanka or the Maldives won't earn you the same brownie points with a Sinhalese or Maldivian accent. Adopting a neutral accent understood worldwide, I am told, is a way to look cultured. Well, overdone to imperfection, it just ends up in a neutered you.

Solution suggested

On return to India, a verbal exam during immigration clearance where a person can be sent back to the countries whose accents they have imbibed than pollute our diction. The only problem is that some sound like nothing anyone has ever heard before, so they might end up getting stuck in transit for the rest of their lives.

Accent SNAFU (Situation Normal, All Fouled Up)

A lady from a South American country, with English as her second (and hardly spoken) language became the most sought-after social diva in Dilli. She spoke in an accent that required an unimaginable amount of concentration to decode every word that toppled out of her mouth. An unsuspecting passerby would assume it to be a meaningful conversation, and be curious to find out what's holding my focus. I for one can't decipher a word, let alone lead such a conversation.

Verdict: All points are scored by our indecipherable South American diva, making her the winner of the popularity championship.

~

My friend, a third-generation Texan of Indian origin has, on occasion, made gatecrashing interesting. Once we went for dinner to a resort hotel, one of the finest in the country. Dressed casually in denims and boots, we decided to burn some calories and digest the *lal maas*—a Rajasthani delicacy cooked in oil and butter—by walking the sprawling lawns after dinner. Our path was lit by fireworks and like moths attracted to light, we flocked to an enclosed area with high security—a royal wedding was underway. My friend with her genuine American drawl decided to put her best foot forward.

Not only were the gates opened for us instantly by the guards, we danced in the *baraat* and have photographs with the immediate family of the groom.

10

The Big 'Three Zero'

If you think that the single woman in her late twenties leads a tormented life, wait till the time bomb ticks to thirty. Thankfully, by now she has already ordered a thicker hide on eBay and wears it with indifference and to be honest, a little glee.

I got a group of single women to draw up a list of pro et contra of being single and in their thirties.

Contra

1. Constant bitching and speculation by other women

The creative storyteller in most married women surfaces when a carefree woman, unlike them, waltzes into their surroundings. She is the only one who needs to be tripped at any possible opportunity by the chorus of married women and what better way to do it than to sing an obscene tune to anyone that bothers to offer them an ear.

This milestone came to me a year back and my ears started ringing with some Chinese whispers which kept fleshing out my very ordinary persona with interesting details. The stories range from adding a decade to my actual age to multiplying the male partners in my life by fifty.

Rumour has it that I have a child—an estranged daughter—whom I don't talk about. When some people comment on her absence, I say she was taken away by an NGO for the abuses I inflicted upon her…and then I wait for their reactions.

2. Reputation given by men

Single, ready to mingle, is the first impression a man in this city gets when they bump into a single woman in her thirties. *Easy* is what she is—easy to get into the sack, easy to get out of one's life, easy to remember and easier to forget.

3. Single and alone

She belongs to an oppressed minority without too many women with whom to celebrate her singledom, resulting in a majority of men, both single and married, forming her inner circle.

Even when she does finally find a soul sister with the same dilemma, their competitive drive over the same man, the same house, the same pair of shoes or the same promotion drives them apart.

We were and still are women in quest of true love, though we may camouflage it with a blatant 'Who needs men, we have it all.' But the truth would have the makings of a reality show guaranteed to generate the highest TRPs.

A girlfriend fought with me and decided to let go of an honest connection over a guy that she had not even met till that fateful date. Well, she was supposed to meet him through a friend and didn't, so I met him and had fun. Does that really qualify as any of the deadly sins?

Teeth were sharpened, knives glazed with poison and a war with no victors was declared.

Moral of the story: no matter what, as single women in their thirties, divided we fall and united we fight.

4. The psychiatric evaluation

A single man in his thirties is a prime catch. A single woman in her thirties is a prime suspect for abnormalities—confidence issues, commitment phobia, emotional flatness, mood swings and in some cases even schizophrenia, or other personality disorders that a recent study (by, let me guess…men?) shows such women are more predisposed to. So it's best to stay away from her.

5. Reproduction challenge

Let's see. You are in your thirties. You give yourself a year to find the right man, a year to date and understand him, a year into marriage to reproduce. By then you will already be in your mid thirties. This is assuming you found the right guy, or God knows you will be stuck in this loop even in your forties. When you hit your fifties, isn't it a great idea to have a teenage kid with high levels of rebellion, ruining your plans of a beachside condo or any other early retirement plans?

So philosophical dilemma—to reproduce or not to reproduce, once over the entire mountain range?

Pros

1. The charm of the wood

Exploration, Enlightenment, Excitement. The world is a candy store! You can put your finger on any man (or woman) you like and call dibs. A new wrapper for a new present every night. A Christmas morning everyday singing exotic carols with hopefully no 'silent nights.' A birthday wish 'cumming' true with every 'blow' of the candle. Your own dream story with a new lead for 'eyes wide open.' For world peace you live, spreading love and spreading for love. A life that's not only beautiful but booty-full!

2. The charm of being wooed

Where there is a single available woman, there is always more than one man in the queue, age and brains no bar.

The matter is not settled at the break of dawn but in the stealth of the night. Duelling pistols are replaced by wads of cash, armour by flattery and horses by sports cars.

Never can she be taken for granted. Never will she let herself be taken for granted. This vixen is no house cat with nothing better to do. Instead, she needs to be hunted.

3. Freedom to...

Eat in bed and sleep on the couch. Like a man.
Leave make-up on the face and lingerie on the floor. Like a pig.
Drink Diet Coke from the can, smear the glassware with lipstick. Like a vamp.
Not put curlers in the hair at night, and not shave the legs. Like a toad.

Drive like you own the road; traffic rules are only for others. Charge in the opposite direction of a one-way road; park parallel without mastering the know-how; take directions at every turn from people who know a shit-all, and try making GPS your best friend. Like a woman.

The only difficulty I faced while doing this piece was finding single women who were willing to admit being in their big 'three zero.' And the ones who did, made me swear on my original black hair to protect their identities.

11

Farmhouse Parties

They are the best and as I am writing this, I am kind of recovering from a hangover thanks to a night of two such parties.

Kindly note, this is not an option for a regular bloke.

'What's in a name?' You're kidding me? Shakespeare wasn't born in the 20th century in Dilli... It's all in the name. If you are born with one of the golden family names, wear enough diamonds to make even me plot robbing you, you have the world at your feet and are capable of pulling together a fiesta like this.

A special occasion is grand, but no occasion is even better. Scattered across Chattarpur, Mehrauli and Rajokri, are acres of well-tended gardens, cobbled pathways and landscaping that make up for the otherwise tortuous journey you have to undertake just to reach one of these destinations.

Unheard-of themes are very popular—pigs fly (literally) for the 'Suckling Pig' theme; Akon comes in with a laser show better than you would have seen in any stadium; the 'Under Construction' theme for a farmhouse under renovation competes with the controversial 'White Parties' or 'Jungle Laws.'

I have walked on stars and tasted candy clouds fed by angels. I have entered the deathly gallows of Hell and met Satan in the plunging fires warming the freezing Dilli winters. I have been a witch and sometimes been bewitched. I have seen nudity in the 'Michelangelo' theme, and the Rajasthani Village of my dreams. I have been to mountain huts and Goan shacks, sat in gondolas under a bridge in Venice. I have danced on the beaches of Ibiza and even managed a snowball fight in the Alps. I have worn bikinis and tiaras, and draped sarees and pyjamas.

All in Dilli, within a radius of 20 km.

Birthdays, anniversaries, Christmas, New Year, Diwali, Holi, Easter, unending pre- and post-wedding parties… been there, done that.

Any more details of these parties and I shall burn my bridges to further invites. Now that I have tasted blood, I would not miss them for the world.

P.S.

1. You can gatecrash so long as you know at least five invited guests. Then you belong in the same circle and all is forgiven.

2. Ensure you are dressed to the hilt and fit in like a piece in a puzzle instead of looking like a puzzle. Remember 'Shine On' is not just a song played by the DJ in these parties.

3. Always have a driver. Parking is a disaster and if you are a woman, or with a woman (covering all bases), those stilettos are a pain in you know what.

4. Ok, this one is for the rare me and you who like to carry a drink in the car (no, I am not encouraging drinking and driving. Refer rule #3), ensure a large glass for the long distance, and a straw for the uneven terrain over which you are sure to bump your head on the roof. Else, you will ruin either your expensive dress or the steering wheel.

5. In case of back-to-back farmhouse parties in the same vicinity, do not exhaust all your conversation subjects; save some for the next party as well as you will be with the same privileged group again.

6. Wear heavy perfumes as you would be meeting and hugging at least 100 people who will be sweating and dancing even when the air-conditioning conks off.

7. Do not feel offended if your parents decide to disown you on your return (if and whenever you do decide to return).

12

House Parties, Punjabi Ishtyle

Some say the glass is half-empty, others say the glass is half-full. And Punjabis say, 'Who cares, so long as the bar is still standing.'

Punjab is a state in India where every person has a similar mindset. Punjabis are not always drunk if that's what you think but by nature they are loud, crazy and sometimes obnoxious creatures. Or let's say that's how my docile Tamilian friend introduces me to an unsuspecting audience.

Without reason, a party is planned, an arrival time fixed, with suggestions to carry sunglasses for the hour at which you may leave. You can invite however many people even if you are not the host. Sometimes you don't even recognise half the people who have invited themselves over. Not that anyone cares. The more the merrier.

We always order liquor by the cases, and food with enough scope for leftovers to help pacify agitated neighbours the next morning.

With special dancing lights, disco balls and a DJ always present, an evening starts with international tunes churned out in the first hour or two. We try to behave and have normal conversations to atone in advance for being rowdy later on on the dance floor. A floating microphone encourages the audience to scream 'Hoy Hoy,' to Punjabi music, and dedications for friends and family, with a dash of profanity is a customary ritual. As for the dance movements, anything goes, since who cares—splits on the floor, B-Boying movements, lifts with men picking up men (!) and women jumping on every piece of furniture sprinkled on the dance floor, preferably with a pole or pillar around it.

Strong family values are part of our Punjabi culture. There is always a dancing Grandpa, a lost kid or a jiving Mum and Dad at the centre with an entire *bhangra* (Punjabi folk dance) party circling them, with surprisingly synchronised movements. When the cult song 'Kala Chashma' (literal translation—dark glasses) is played, your accessories in the car come in handy even before the crack of dawn.

The food is largely predictable with the delicious pairing of *tangri kebabs* (roasted chicken legs) unmistakably hand-fed to everyone, and whiskey, with butter-chicken for main course. By now, no more polite sipping of drinks; only a boisterous gulping competition to the screams of 'Bottoms-up.'

Mind you, the evening is not over till at least one drama unfolds to make it memorable—a drunk, sobbing girl on the staircase, a puking wife locked in the powder room, youngsters with uncontrollable-hormones disease making out in the backyard, an uncle passed out on the couch and occasionally behind it, or a couple abusing each other in the parking lot.

If you have understood all of the above, and been through the initiation rites, you qualify for hosting a Punjabi Party with 200 per cent attendance guaranteed.

13

The Married Darlings

Till homicide does us apart, and maybe, not even then.

Our married darlings are often spotted with a pained expression—a continuation I guess of a typical day of separate lives, kids, daily chores and over exposure to one another. Then there is the picking of the nose, the flossing of teeth, the morning bad breath, the occasional tantrums, the fight to be always right. And none of this can be set right with sweaty hugs straight after the gym. The non-existent I in the *we*, let's face it, is always a priority.

I know of some couples who do not talk to each other unless there is a third party mediation they have invited as a guest or taken hostage under the false pretense of a fun night. Complains and previous night's fight confessions make you a referee where eventually only you lose the five hours of your life that will never come back. And they gain a shrink for the rest of their lives who charges by the peg.

Another variety, who offer you (sometimes money as well) to take their wife/ husband out so they can finally get an evening of debauchery to butcher their own reputation.

My very own friend paid me a thousand rupees to give a lap-dance to her husband as a distraction technique to buy an extra hour or two of clubbing. But she is the generous one you see. Another girlfriend of the same group only offers me fifty rupees to stop her husband from taking her home. It's more of a charity case where the sight of her being dragged without her will while she is digging in her heels all the way to the car-park is a pathetic sight where you think what a horrid man she is married to. So what if it's 5 a.m. and he starts his work day at 9 a.m.? *He* should understand.

Then come the most avoidable couples who, every time they step out, complain about their lives to all. The verbal bantering converting into physical battering. The dramatic slap, the classic drink on the face, the graceful tripping executed by an extended leg. No, not with each other but with anyone who dares to talk to the spouse. The dog in the manger attitude—'I don't want my wife, so how dare you?'

But the winner is...a wife begging and pleading for secrecy about her earlier tantrum that you have witnessed, now that the husband is holding her arm. (In case you wish to speak of a husband doing the same, just change the pronouns and nouns appropriately.) An endless supply of alcohol for the night buys the silence of a not so innocent lamb.

Relationship or Relationshit, the façade is very important. The tag and ring are a must. Let's face it, you don't want the entire city talking about you (even if it does).

But every once in a while, when I see a couple truly in love, I want to jump off my chair, fling aside my stilettos and hug them. My faith is restored in the institution of marriage on such occasions but unfortunately that belief is usually short-lived.

A lot of my friends have been through a full cycle of marriage, divorce and back to their single selves. Some with the vow of remaining in 'Singleton Heaven,' and others now somewhat wiser (?) from past experiences, still trying to find the right one.

But mostly I see in each married person's eyes regret for being in there just as I see in a single person's eyes the regret of having let it go.

As for me, the grey area of living it up is good enough.

14

What is Mobile Number?

Now that's a common denominator for one and all. If your update doesn't change every two hours, if your status doesn't tell everyone details from the number of sugar cubes or the quantity of Aspartame in your morning coffee to the exact mixology technique of your nightcap, you are a social disgrace and the world knows you as nothing but a loser. All your expensive and exotic holidays are gone down the drain.

A private, intimate poker game at a media baron's house is a must-flaunt even if the host is nowhere in the country and his mansion has a padlock.

So, how do you balance the art of eating and getting the right display/Page 3 pictures of the act?

I meet a very dear friend of mine (you shall soon know why) twice a year but her social networking keeps me abreast of her life. I might not know my schedule for the day but I definitely know the number of courses she plans to order for dinner, in which of her favourite restaurants, accompanied by whom all... I envy her zest and fervour for the social frenzy that her life is. It makes me wonder if I can bribe her mailman for just a few of those invitations. But every time I manage an evening out with her, I end up with a throbbing jaw after smiling and pouting with her at the camera constantly held by her husband.

6 easy ways of enhancing your social networking

1. Add a middle name or change your last name to a singer, a designer or an actor's screen name. Add to it adjectives defining you as sexy or shy, a cutie or a pumpkin. Ensure beauty does not lie in the eyes of the beholder but is a vision on their handsets.

2. Update your display pictures against carefully chosen backdrops with appropriate captions: hotel lobbies with extensive flower arrangements—'leaving home'; standing on escalators—'en route to my room'; holding hand-showers in your friend's hotel suite—'time for a bath'; sneaking into the Club Class of an aircraft—'Ah! My bed tonight'; watering plants on your morning walk in a community garden—'My roses aren't blooming.' And please *never* leave out the display picture of a test drive in a new sports car. And we can put our heads together for the caption.

Once you get a hang of all this, your pretentious life is all sorted. Believe me it is all sorted, since no one has the time to verify your claims.

3. Be a social stalker. Invest in handsets with a high-quality camera so it looks less conspicuous. Look for parties and clubs, fashion shows and events. Map out your evening, preferably with a friend, and click pictures with all. Use one everyday and be the one socially stalked after some time. If you get a celebrity from Mumbai—*Jackpot*. When you mention you are on your way to your fourth party of the night, no one will know you were uninvited to all. Your picture updates with the host will make four wrongs into one great social right.

4. Public display of affection is essential for every married or committed man. Occasionally, it works for women too. Being a family man or woman gives you license to flirt in the open. Ensure your friends are on first-name basis with your spouse, your kids and even your pets.

5. Broadcast to the world you are missing your wife who is travelling. You would then have already taken the first step towards casting your net for the night.

6. Display your sense of humour. My favourite technique is shamelessly plagiarising from Twitter, Facebook and Google funny pictures. You can also quote a Barney Stinston or a Charlie Sheen to show you are in with it. Be careful to avoid 'Friends' (too commonplace) but the current season of 'Big Bang Theory' is good enough. If you follow those two or three simple steps, you shall become

an intelligent person overnight, a deep thinker with layers of mystery. Show off the international experience acquired through channel surfing and Internetworking.

Your mobile should be such that updates about your recently acquired or upcoming handset model becomes breaking news in itself.

15

Dilli, Not New Delhi

Dilli has a zonal caste system that would be difficult to abolish. And to establish what is superior, you have to define what is inferior.

For most Dilli-ites (a terminology as important as Member of Parliament), the buzzword is South Dilli—the summit of luxury, the bubble of prosperity, the concentration of the elite, the haven of the 'haves.' Ok, let me add to that Lutyen's Dilli as well. Then comes the rustic, ill-mannered, tacky and not so genteel North and West Dilli, I suppose. East Dilli? What East Dilli? Are you talking about that area coked with industrial centres?

A rented apartment in Lajpat Nagar is better than a bungalow in Punjabi Bagh. A farmhouse with no infrastructure in some village in Chattarpur is in with, a row boat as a must during monsoons. Put together, a mini palace in Civil Lines with acres of lawns, and the Dilli University beyond, can't hold a candle to that coveted Chattarpur property.

Why, a socialite who snubs her social peers, coined a phrase that made my brows leap out of my forehead—

EW Dilli. Stands for East and West Dilli. And her qualification for both—'Ewww.'

So pronounced is this hierarchy that it took me a while to publically accept that I didn't belong *originally* to the posh South Dilli where you must store water between 3 and 4 p.m. or 3 and 4 a.m. in case you want to ensure enough water in the cisterns and the recycled mineral water bottle.

A popular question asked by everyone in this city is 'Where do you live?' The wrong pin code means code blue leading to social hara-kiri, and indifference heaped on the less fortunate, socially deprived 'have-nots.'

And if you think I am spinning yarns, in the next snooty gathering, try dropping names of residential black holes like Patparganj, Rohini, Pitampura, Daryaganj, Laxmi Nagar or Rajouri Garden and enjoy people reaching out for their smelling salts. We may go to the same school, Ivy League college, office, movie theatre, night club, but... And may the Lord's prayer help the inhabitants of suburban Ghaziabad and Faridabad.

Now I was born and raised for the first 25 years of my life in Model Town, a part of the North Dilli Zone, with my family originally hailing from Chandni Chowk. So what does that make me?

16

Chronicles of a Bartender

When Oscar Wilde said, 'Work is the curse of the drinking class,' he never knew a bartender. I, on the other hand, have a fair amount of expertise in this field with over a decade of memories that I wouldn't trade for the world.

My current ambition—labour for liquor.

As a 19-year-old straight out of school, being in the limelight and the glamour of nightlife were very powerful draws. The first time I held a bottle to pour a drink, was the first time I fell in love...with alcohol. And we still seem to be going steady.

The sexist law of the times forbade a woman from taking up this noble profession and helping people find happiness. Too bad, since it didn't create enough fear of being behind the prison gates, so I bashed on regardless... Hedonism became the buzzword, for them, for me.

While a good drunk may not make a good bartender, being a good bartender made me a great drunk.

If earlier I was always home before 9 p.m. when the curfew hours kicked in, I opted for a career that now required me to *leave* home at that controversial hour.

It was like a stage waiting for the star performer in me who would have her subjects bowing down for a drink or two. Perhaps that was because I was the only woman bartender, and always had a host of guests queuing in front of me—some leching and the others that I couldn't quite keep my own eyes off. My favourites were Bollywood fare and international cricketers at farmhouse parties that Dilli is famous for. I am itching to divulge names of the celebrity eyes I have flirted with while they were under influence of my charming extra dose of vodka in their drinks.

A drink or two never makes your dreams come true. Perhaps a bottle or two would.

I can't say I was born into this culture but I definitely grew up or, more graphically, drowned in it.

Once, I looked into the eyes of one of the Bollywood 'Khans' and forgot everything around me. Both the drink in my hand and I started drooling till I was kicked on my shin by a fellow bartender. The next 10 minutes were spent cleaning the floor…

Another time, it was the Australian cricket team, with a man whose poster I used to idol worship in my house as a kid. While he was calling the security (as I wouldn't get my arms off him), I was also exchanging phone numbers with a budding young team-mate of his who is an international force to reckon with now.

Yet another time was this hen party for one of the very prominent Dilli family's daughter, with my first experience of watching naked male glory in the form of male strippers pole dancing.

I relished five drunken wedding proposals around the bar counter in three months which were thankfully forgotten the next morning.

With a bottle in my hands, I acquired quite a few fans.

But mind you, the school of bartending does qualify the bartender to distinguish the drunk from the plain dumb.

Dilli society has globe-trotting geniuses and self-proclaimed connoisseurs who can't differentiate between their whiskeys and cognacs after the third drink. The favourite that night in a bar with the rarest blends and oldest malts was Johnny Walker Blue Label with half soda and half water. The fanciest bottle of 'Dimple' stole a march over the sedate single-barrel hand-crafted Scotch. Hotels and bars constantly replace their most expensive whiskeys with even more expensive ones since the right side of the menu must impress your 'friends,' even at the cost of your own pockets.

Once, in a farmhouse party, I was serving my dreaded Mathematics professor from school days who disregarded the skill required for my trade and cited me as an example to explain to his own children how the lack of education could destroy ones potential. Well, at least I considered myself constructive enough to *set* a bad example.

Unfortunately, my wit deserted me when my own parents popped up across the bar counter. You have to understand it was a shock born out of ignorance as they had absolutely no idea of this passion of mine (I was supposed to be at a joint study group all this while). Mortified and disgruntled, I saw shame pouring out of every single pore of their bodies shaken with embarrassment and garnished with a slice of fear for my well-being. It took numerous verbal sessions, family discussions and occasional therapy (for my parents) to finally accept my little twist in their 'sobriety.'

17

Boys Night Out

He is the Alpha Male. The Monarch. It's his world and we are only visitors. The Rich Single Dilli Boy finally grows up to a Not So Single Dilli Boy. He has had a wedding which packed in six days of festivities, took six months to plan, 600 people to execute and six crores of his father's hard-earned money.

The fidelity clause as discussed, unfortunately lasts no more than six days.

Congratulations if the marriage actually survives six months or felicitations to either party for lifting the Oscar for deception.

I happened to work with one such man. A sweet, chiselled man in his mid-twenties, he was slightly under-confident (sometimes he stuttered during board meetings) and could only impose his sexuality in the garb of power. In a nutshell, sexual harassment at workplace.

When he made a controversial offer to me, I must confess, I was more curious than offended. His beautiful bride of eight months was sitting at home for him. It had been a Hindi-movie style love marriage: generations of feuding Punjabi families, tears and at least one song-and-dance sequence of the lovebirds eventually melting hardened hearts, with both sides burying age-old differences to mount *the wedding of the decade*. His love for his wife when they were together was suffocating to witness.

When I questioned the rationale behind for his preposition, the closet stud said, 'Suppose your favourite colour is white. Hence, you pack your wardrobe with loads of white. Then you start missing the reds, greens and blues. So, a bright tie, a coloured pair of cuff-links and cherry shoes never hurt. It's not like you still don't like your white or your wife.' Sounds logical, and no, I wasn't the victim. Instead, got him to undress his interesting and dysfunctional mind.

~

Married 'Boys' Night Out. Hurrah! Every such night is a fantasy fabricated by a man who would rather be a boy looking to better his 'score.'

Dream Scenario

With his group of besties, happy as a gopher in soft dirt, he plans a giddi-up night ahead where he dons his cowboy hat and gallops into the sunset on his steed to enter a shady saloon where boobilicious young maids carrying beer pitchers, all queuing up to cover him with kisses. An evening of lewd behaviour, catcalls and snide remarks, each 'boy,' crooked as a dog's hind leg is led to secret boudoirs by brazen floozies to do some Yeee-Haaaw.

Real Scenario 1

Five married men gather to thrash out a philosophical dilemma—which bar would grant them access without their women in tow. Once this dilemma is sorted, they do nothing but stick to their theme. *Boys Night Out*—roar before you explore. With jokes high on testosterone, it's a series of bottoms-up, with not much else packed in.

Real Scenario 2

A group of five middle-aged bald overweight men order beer. Completely out of their depth, these rotten apples stand in a corner and ogle at the forbidden fruit till they instigate fights and have to be plucked out from the fruit basket by well-meaning bar bouncers.

No group hunting in this sport. Carefully camouflaged, the hyena approaches the lamb stealthily. Don't want to be led to the slaughterhouse by wifey, you see.

Usually, these indiscretions are ignored by the spouses as part and parcel of the whole marriage deal. However, a daring 10 per cent, in their Louboutins demand the floor they stomp on, along with the house it's built over, with the driveway, lawns, the Rottweilers and the staff thrown in.

Now, we are talking 10 per cent of annual marriages in this circle. Hmmm. Gosh. The problems these boys create for the poor event manager planning a guest list. The columns for Mrs. and Mr. become obsolete every quarter.

I had moved out of the city for a year but kept visiting it at least a weekend a month. Yet, the number of faux pas I committed each time was phenomenal…

Me: It's so nice to see you. How are the kids doing?
Him: Don't know. My wife has them now.

Me (over the phone): Hello, I lost your husband's number and wanted to schedule a meeting.
Her (over the phone): I don't have a husband anymore. (CLICK)

Me: So, what's new?
Him: You kidding? No one. Not since my wife caught me red-handed and a popular blog wrote about it.

Me: You know Mr. X was caught cheating on his wife last month? I wonder who that was.
Her: As if you don't know it was me.

Me: Hope you brought your wife along?
Him: Yes. The new one.

And here's the best of the pick:

Her: I can't get through to my husband.
Me: I'll call.
Her: That's not his number.
Me: But it's the one he gave me. (*Oops!*)

The couple separated a fortnight later.

18

When a Woman Says, 'I Do Too'

To be fair, 'doing it' is not only a man's prerogative. Some women feel they ought to discreetly reciprocate their husband's kindness though that may not be the only excuse.

A married woman, with a husband who is deft at giving the glad eye and much more, can rightfully crave a bit of attention, a little tending, a look with a hint of lust, to once again become the girl who can make hearts go arrhythmic with a few seductive moves.

The prospect and potential is thrilling—for the woman, for her handsome prey, for the over-possessive husband, for all the friends who 'know' and are willing to take a shot at it too.

But unlike the score card maintained by men, this woman may merely have her feet kissed, and occasionally a bit more too, under the mistletoe and sometimes under a duvet. Add to that sexting and plans of more secret rendezvous.

This business is translucent, and above moral reproach, so let's not make this woman a Scarlet O'Hara! She is only doing what comes naturally to her—being Lolita at the drop of the hat, and sometimes a bit more.

Now look, it's alright to break the shackles for a limited time just to put them on again. Knowing you have the key makes you feel less of a prisoner. It makes you a willing hostage who can enjoy the marital goodies too.

When alone, go full steam and charm that handsome bloke at the counter. And if the husband is around, suspend yourself from his arm to underscore your successful marriage. These carefully executed manoeuvres ought to remove and create ambiguity at the same time. Deception gives a great high.

Sometimes, the real action with lights, camera and the works, only unfolds in foreign lands without the matrimonial appendage. Getaway excuses are legion—a girly vacation, a business trip, a visit to one's hometown, a much-needed yogic retreat...

And for unfathomable reasons, I am the unanimously elected Miss Shining Armour to accompany the wayward ladies on these trips (danger needs an ally). And since with great power comes great responsibility, away from home turf, mine comes with huge vodkas, great food, and vows of secrecy.

19

Alcohol *ke* Cider Effects

Ever wondered about those momentous decisions, which seem just perfect taken in the stealth of the night while the liver is going into overdrive, but seem quite delirious when the sun shines outside your window, while you nurse a blasted headache that makes you want to shoot all the protagonists of the previous night's potboiler?

Waking up in the morning or afternoon next to a guy you can't remember; having a one-hour conversation you can't recollect; professing undying love for someone you would otherwise not consider remotely likeable—most of us have been there in. Alcohol sets everything right just as the 12 hour aftermath plays party-pooper.

So, with my vast hands-on experience, here's a quiz for everyone—15 questions to be answered with a simple 'Yes' or 'No':

Question 1

Three drinks down, do you wish to call the last guy or the girl who showered even an ounce of attention on you?

Question 2
Ever written off someone completely and yet made the mistake of somehow trying to set things right one last time?

Question 3
An instant attraction blossomed in a bar when someone flashed a 28 teeth smile at you (not counting the wisdom teeth here)?

Question 4
Do you believe everyone loves you because you're just so hot?

Question 5
Ever jumped on a table in your bleeding lipstick and torn stockings and danced like nobody was watching till you realised the next day that everybody, in fact, had, and how?

Question 6
Unanimously designated by drunken pals as the safest driver in India, when challenged, you have driven 200 km to and back from Agra at 4 a.m. just to prove a point?

Question 7
Ever snatched the microphone during a stage performance and sung a song seemingly better than a pro?

Question 8
Ever ordered the most expensive champagne on the menu hoping everyone saw you ordering it, opening it, drinking it *And* dancing with the empty bottle on your head?

Question 9
Ever grabbed a bouncer's collar in the club where he has had a couple of dozens lined up to beat the crap out of you? (Because I have!)

Question 10
At social dos, ever jumped into every picture being clicked whether you were welcome in it or not? (More so with strangers.)

Question 11
Ever had verbal diarrhoea, with your deepest darkest secrets tumbling out in front of total strangers?

Question 12
Ever believed you could pick up your drunken, overweight friend, sometimes two, single-handedly and carry him to his car in the parking lot in the basement without thinking it could entail an eventual trip to the emergency room for an IV drip for yourself?

Question 13
Pretending to be the richest and smartest person around,

have you ever paid for everyone's drink even if you couldn't remember their names?

Question 14
Ever given your two-penny wisdom to someone not drunk enough to follow it, and not remember being their mentor the next day?

Question 15
Ever said, 'I love you' more than twice in a single night and not meant it even once?

If your answer is 'Yes' for more than ten questions, there is nothing extraordinary about you. You are just one of us. And if your answer is 'No' for more than ten questions, congratulations, you are a superhero, and this planet is not for you.

~

Alcohol *ke* Cider Effects

With drinks in both hands
Underpants over the pants,
Everyone feels like Cider Man!
Cider Man, Cider Man.

Spins a yarn, any size
Charms the ladies 'n' the guys.

Then he'd love to take you home
Which he says is just like Rome
He sure is Cider Man.

He's very strong on the 'Bud,'
With gallons of alcohol in his blood.
Can he swig a bottoms up
And still use a pick-up 'Wassup?'
C'mon Cider Man, Cider Man.

In the chill of the night
She wears a sheath so light
Tequila through the shots
Makes the weather and her so hot
Grab her Cider Man, Cider Man.

Wealth and fame he has them all
He lives for the brag and the late night brawl
To him, life is a big bang up
Whenever there's a hang up
Well done Cider Man, Cider Man!

20

The Social Have(s) and Have Not(s)

It has less to do with money (only), and more to do with your ability to collect followers. It's about the number of heads you can turn and kisses you blow when you walk down the aisle on your way to the hub of the social altar, all the while waving your hand and making small inconsequential talk.

The aim: Getting devotees waiting to be noticed by you so you get noticed by all.

You can earn or buy them, steal or, at times, borrow them, whatever comes easier.

A few years ago, I accompanied a dear reporter friend to cover a party at a private lounge of a night club. I knew all the guests and I can bet they knew my name too. However, I could have been a wall no one notices. So no smiles, and no hugs. With all that iciness around, I would have done better to walk into a morgue for warmth.

The hostess was a Bollywood family torch-bearer who had recently moved to Dilli after her marriage. The lady barely acknowledged my presence till my international sports champion date walked in, from whom she sought acknowledgement. Only then did the status quo change. The world revolved around me but on the axis of a big question mark on my worth. What followed was an evening of gushing and mindless chatter, making me want to turn back the clock to the times of the pre-Om silence.

As I looked around the grand hall, having gone through loneliness, rejection to being the belle of the ball, I realised that not many had earned their admirers for their charm or social skills.

So how do you arrive in Dilli?

You can hire Dilli's top hostess to host a party and call her friends. Sure, it doesn't come cheap but surely a smile will be exchanged in the next encounter and push up your social graph. You will get a party that is talked about for a month. The hired help will buy herself a customised Bugatti, and Dilliwalas shall get free booze yet again.

Or

You can buy a media personality development programme. Look, it's cheaper to have your face plastered in the cities' leading dailies with mostly exotic women in the wings. Your birthdays, weddings, anniversaries and birthdays of your children shall all be covered in those bought-up pages.

Or

Try direct purchase. Have the whole bar on the house just to feed everyone you feel is worth knowing. There is no debt like the debt of a bar bill. And should you do it regularly, others shall be coerced into adding your name to their guest lists as well.

Eventually, the world (I mean Dilli...what's the difference?) will know the sweet person that you are and make sure you live happily ever after in Dilli.

21

The Nillionaire Club

You guessed it right. People with little or no money but great survival technique are this club's lifetime members.

Unlike in a club, he never hangs around with his ilk, and survives by spacing himself out in different groups. Yes, it's usually a man, a confirmed guest for any occasion that comes free. Women never fall in this category, you see, they only rise in popularity.

For this Club Card holder, it's essential to maintain his turf and prevent another one from encroaching on his well-chosen territory. Generous friends usually do not support more than one epicurean nillionaire in a group.

These friends are usually ones who can afford parties in their homes, hi-end restaurants, night clubs, holiday destinations, dish out passes to the right events and offer rides in cars he wishes to be seen in.

In return, the nillionaire pledges lifelong loyalty not only to you but your entire family, and even offers to take your sick dog to the vet. He dedicates his life to giving you emotional support and dollops of understanding. He stands by you through thick and thin, defends you and is offended by any disrespect shown towards you. In brief, your personal champion.

At a restaurant, when the bill is served up, unfailingly his hand reaches for the wallet behind the butt, but lingers there till the bill is settled. His entire life is a strategy: when to appear, when to disappear, where to put up an appearance, how to handle the ramifications. He has to endure a lot of snide remarks but that's small change for a swig of free beer.

But there's a bigger problem that awaits him. How to date?

The Dilli woman expects (and *deserves*) a royal treatment. How to deal with that without loosening your purse strings?

I once made the mistake of introducing a friend to him. Unlike a regular Dilli girl, she didn't expect any fancy frills as she could afford those on her own. Nillionaire, however, assumed that any plans with her meant he would have to fork out for the goose and the gander. For a while he decided to walk at a tangent to her each time he saw her.

Accompanying my friend (a night-club devotee who worships her Vodka) for an outing that didn't come free, was simply out of question. It had to be one of the boring hosted parties, events or nothing. What's more, his booty calls came post 2 a.m., when my friend was happily drunk in order to reap the benefits of the seed he couldn't sow.

Yeah, you guessed it. Nillionaire is still a freeloader and my friend has enriched her stock of expletives.

22

Bar Brawls

A night out in Dilli is not complete without a bar or a brawl, or both.

I have long witnessed such fights (at least once in five club evenings) but let me make one thing clear—neither am I the one fighting nor am I the cause of the fight. One look at me, and you know I am not lying. I am just the innocent bystander.

Addicted to partying till six in the morning, I do get to witness human beings, in 108 manifestations, sometimes in a single evening.

Dilli is a city with illusory power in the hands of all, power backed either by money or relatives in the Upper House. A discussion not in your favour, becomes an argument in no time, ending in fights of bloody proportions—typically one of the marvellous effects of alcohol.

I have seen ordinary mortals transform into great warriors faster than the speed of light. But I just do not match up. Once when I tried to duck to avoid a blow, I got punched in the gut. What was I doing in that melee?

Witness for non-prosecution, and failed ombudsman. Since then, I either crouch in a corner or run to to my car to make a quick getaway.

I have even had a gun pointed at my head and a broken bottle pointed at my stomach. Both were mystical experiences.

Talking in detail of a single incident means disregarding the other glorious pow-wows. So let me share with you the traditional drink-to-black-eye cycle.

You drink, you become the king of the world. If your inflated ego is pricked by some jerk, God help him. Shoulders rise, chest expands, nostrils flare, muscles twitch, adrenaline pumps. An aggressive verbal dialogue is followed by you grabbing his collar and kneeing his groin. Groups of friends come to defend both sides and a war rages. Then the cops arrive. Both parties have tea in the police station. A compromise is reached. Usually the lesser group changes its haunt. And the greater group has breakfast at the Hyatt (that's where I may step back in again).

And this one not-so-fun fight provides fodder for gossip for an entire month with various versions for you to choose from.

Please note: This is Dilli, and everyone is a winner in all fights.

23

The Beautiful Beast

Now and here in Dilli exists a beautiful, stylish, epitome of looks. At the sight of this Punjabi with Afghan blood, and a muscled body from the cow-rich state of Haryana, my pulse shoots up to 178 per minute without that being the sign of delirium cordis. This beauty causes tongues to roll out, mouths to salivate and unleashes an uncontrollable urge to explore skin...till he opens his mouth.

Dressed as a combination of Elvis Presley and John Travolta, he breaks out in profanities in the local language laced with a Haryanvi accent. MC, BC and a few other private body parts are emphasised in every conversation. The combination is phrased in a manner that is more hilarious than offensive. Even a scary phrase like *gaand pe thappad* in actuality is not that violent: '*gaand*' means arse and '*thappad*' is a slap. That adds up to *spanking*.

The words uttered by the deep, grungy voice (I use these here for purely educational purposes), include '*bhenchod*' (sister-fucker), '*madarchod*' (mother-fucker), '*bhosdike*' (I still don't know what it means), the ever so popular '*chutiya*' (cunt) and *gaandu* (asshole). And believe me, he used those words as punctuations—space, comma, colon, semi-colon, hyphen, full stop, exclamation mark, question mark, even inverted commas.

So here is a ready-reckoner:

bakchodi: when men get together to gossip
bharwa: someone who sides with your enemy
bhenchod: anyone who makes a big mistake
bhosdi mein gaya: extremely complicated matter
buddha khoosad: respect for the elderly
chutiya: see above
dimaag ki maa behen: screwing the mind
gaand faadu: a difficult task to be accomplished; a person who accomplishes it
gaand fati: terribly scared of what the future holds
gaandu: see above
kahaan gaand mara raha hai: checking on the whereabouts of your dear ones
kutta kameena: term of endearment for friends
lund se: lack of regret, guilt or remorse for your actions
maa chudi padi hai: busy beyond words; life gone haywire
madarchod: see above

More after you have digested these.

Once I was over at a very well-educated friend's place. In my presence, he yakked with his uncle over the phone for just a couple of minutes. At last count, it was 11 '*bhenchods*.'

This is a talent programmed in the DNA of most Dilliwalas. What bothers me though is their other linguistic handicaps. Stringing together two correct sentences seems as tough as a tightrope walk. A favourite pick-up line from an admirer would shed some light on what I mean, 'I want to launch my friendship on you.' Houston, we do have a problem.

For relief from such a rich linguistic fare, I travelled to the Southern states of India where their greetings alone had me in splits. Stepping out of the aircraft, on my first trip to Hyderabad, Andhra Pradesh, I was received by a hotel representative who greeted me with folded hands and '*Randi*'—welcome in Telegu. But more was yet to *come* when in Chennai, Tamil Nadu, the bell-boy in a hotel lobby greeted me with a '*Vanakkam*.' I almost said 'Anytime, anywhere, hon' till I realised that meant *Namaskar* in Tamil.

Be that as it may, will someone please tell me why 'motherfucker' is hip and '*madarchod*' isn't, or why 'asshole' is cool and '*gaandu*' isn't?

24

A Small-Town Girl

A nice young girl came to Dilli from Chandigarh, not that small a town, about five hours drive from Delhi.

To begin with, it was a small apartment, fun roommates, simple smiley magnets and family pictures all over the refrigerator. Then she met her prince charming (already married), moved into his apartment and acquired the life of the rich and infamous.

A few months down the line, as expected, a new flavour caught our rich boy's fancy.

Out on the road, a thirst for the velvet life made her an easy target for the vultures who made propositions not so easy to decline. Soon, she got sucked into the muck without putting up a fight. What was she after?

Furs on her back?

Villas annually leased out for her?

Diamonds in her locker?

Trips to St. Moritz?

And what about integrity? Missing in action?

No, I don't mean to dispense a moral science lesson here. We all make mistakes. Life doesn't come with a set of instructions. By the time she realised the missing piece, self loathing had already set in. She bottled it up inside her and when she couldn't hide it any more, it showed on her physically bloated being.

This city has a habit, unfortunately, of branding you, especially if you are a woman. Heard of *The Scarlet Letter*, haven't you. Both, the X *and* the Y chromosome bearers pitch in generously for the pillory.

Down and out in the social gutters, as she struggled for support, she drowned herself in alcohol and other forms of illegal intoxicants, making herself even more dependent on those she was running away from.

Then, one day, she was ready to redefine herself. She would be what she wanted to be, and not how she was perceived by others, picking up in the process the pieces of her life, and weeding out the pinpricks on the road to self-discovery.

For a *fallen* woman, *redeeming* herself is an uphill task, and usually must take place in full public view.

But no such thing is applicable to our *big-town girl* or the *fallen* man.

25

Big-Town Girl

From big cities with big dreams comes a big girl to make it big. Great lifestyle, big cars, big house. She wants it all big. She wants the controversial and most desired 'Mr. Big' who is tall and dark. Handsome is good, but 'has some' is even better. There is no need for him to fit the bill as long as he can pay all the bills. He should be in ideal fiscal shape even if low on physical fitness. She prays every night for only one thing to stay up…the stock market.

She works as a crew member with an airline, or as an intern with a fashion house, sells big cars or works in five-star hotels—anywhere where she is kept in 'mink' condition.

She puts herself on display like an Arab Stallion that goes to the Lawrence that bids the highest. Sometimes this bid continues 'after sale' too when she discovers this Lawrence has a friend who can offer more.

She makes her living out of loving.

Her passion for antique men ends with hefty settlements. After that she *mines* her own business.

'Dough or Die' is her battle cry.

So, grow up and be a Big Town Boy. You know this honey comes only for money.

26

Naarad Muni

Not an endangered species by any stretch of imagination. One in every three people you encounter in Dilli's social dos qualifies, man or woman.

True to the mythological character that they epitomise, their lives revolve around a Social God where His (?) name is dropped in every second sentence. Not blind faith but a calculated move to climb the 'stairway to social heaven.'

Past masters of gossip, you can have hours and hours of fun conversation with them as they prey on you and suck you dry of all the gossip they feed on, only to use that against you.

Once they tank up on the not so expensive and easily acquired gossip, they warm themselves on the fires burning between the forever feuding you and me.

One such person is a self-proclaimed Dilli A-lister who is invited to most places and found everywhere. As expected, the claim to fame is a Social God at the top of the pyramid that you don't want to offend. His charm, flattery and the fear of what he says about you never makes you want to turn your back upon him. Moreover, what if he doesn't say anything about you and you discover you are not talked about at all?

No one likes him but everyone enjoys him, especially if he has something to say about someone you don't like.

He has a finger in every pie due to his illegal connections. He will sell you a car, a restaurant concept or an evening at the bar.

A termite wrecking Dilli's entrails, even when he is visible no one attempts a pest control job on him—we are precariously balanced on the bark of the same tree he infests.

27

Get Out of My Way

It's easier, more convenient and entertaining, especially in a city like Dilli. Especially in a night club.

Sticks and stones may break my bones but standing in the way of the 'do you know who I am?' will most definitely break more than what can be put back together by an orthopaedic department.

Educated in top universities around the world, they need to enroll in finishing schools to teach them simple manners. I have personally reminded some of these *khandani* (from well-established families) blokes of their background when they have stooped to levels of black holes, with their colourful vocabulary further embellished with popular adjectives, delivered in a tone which makes me want to pulverise them. The shorter, uglier, and richer they are, the bigger their need to define themselves as *the man*.

I was once managing a bar entrance, with a bouncer standing next to me, when a loud Dilli boy walked right into him and started yelling—how dare lowlife like us block his path. From the London School of Economics, this alumnus also showed how chivalrous he was by ensuring I was walking ahead of him even if he had to resort to brute force and physically push me to lead the way. That's not where it ended; that's where it began. He then looked around to earn accolades from his peers who actually applauded his 'illness.' A warm hug awaited him from the owner of the bar who raised a toast to the showdown with a flute of champagne.

Then comes a variety who claim to get you fired in two seconds. These ones are almost always related to the bar owners through the twenty million people living in this city. With your career in jeopardy, if you dare to call their bluff, you may win 99.9 per cent of the time.

But you don't attain nirvana each night till Daddy's name is dropped. Once, a Mr. Hotshot's son started screaming his Daddy's name even before he and his courtiers had entered the bar. One security chap was made to run amok looking for me to ensure His Holiness was granted access. I relished this momentary sway I held over him. Mr. Hotshot's son was at my mercy. Hey, in my defence, I have a right to amuse myself too, and there was the drink in my hand to finish. Now I rest my case.

Another time, my own butt got a special feeler from a boy, of not more than 20, in a club that I was managing. A part of me was flattered by this rare honour of being singled out by a younger man for his attention, but then better sense prevailed. I asked him politely to step out, and lectured him on how this was unacceptable behaviour. Red-faced, he blared like a broken horn to remind me whose blood ran in his alcoholic veins—a politician so powerful and old that it was obvious he couldn't have desired, let alone sired anything in the last 80 years.

And believe me, I have also had the pleasure of receiving a direct descendant of Chengis Khan at the bar.

~

A serene evening, an al fresco candlelight dinner, the company of educated people (mostly)...what else could I have asked for? A little spice perhaps in my otherwise healthy but bland dinner. Heard of 'Wish carefully, it just may come true?' Well it did.

In the form of a woman thrice my size.

In the form of language I am yet to familiarise myself with.

At such a decibel that four adjoining restaurants could enjoy the debacle and follow every word.

All for an entrance denied to a night club weeks ago.

On another occasion, I was maybe more than a few drinks down when a guy I refused entry to, shoved the gate managers aside only to bump into me. *High* on life in the capital, I held my ground. This Berlin Wall I tell ya wasn't falling so easily. Before I knew, I was threatened with a gun.

Ideal reaction? Run for your life.

My reaction? I burst out laughing.

Turning red in the face, the goon asked me why I found a threat to my life amusing. Well it was. He was huge and there were three of them against me, a single twig trying to ward off a storm. Everyone around me started laughing too. That's when I woke up from my delusional safety, made a beeline for the back gate, got into my car and hid in my house for next three days.

28

When I Was a Pushover

This is the true story of a convicted felon out on bail who partied in this city.

Yes. I was present.

Yes. I met him.

Yes. He was present in our CCTV footage.

Yes. It was a mistake.

But, whose?

Mr. Felon committed a heinous crime in the 1990s. Then he was arrested, released, convicted and granted parole to look after his ailing mother (she was making political appearances everyday; he was jaywalking in nightclubs each day of his parole).

The mystery of that night unravels with every twisted fold of the origami of the male psyche.

It wasn't the vigilance of our Dilli Police that sniffed out Mr. Felon.

It was the chief cop's son's fear of peeing in his pants that made him call his Daddy. Originally, the cops didn't come looking for Mr. Felon. They came to scare Mr. Felon's friend, Mr. Bombastic, who is quite accomplished in bar brawls and had scared the chief cop's son during a fight in a neighbouring club, the latter, tail between legs, having fled from there. And of all the bars in the world, they had to walk into the one where I worked.

Mr. Bombastic's table was already reserved. Introduced to Mr. Felon at the crowded entrance, I didn't place him as his bail was not a public announcement and really we weren't on the lookout for him. Or that's my excuse.

Now I am wiser. I have a chart in my room which will put the list of wanted in a cop station to shade.

Instead of coming to this city and quietly enjoying himself as would have been a logical, even though an illegal act, Mr. Felon came with Mr. Bombastic as a friend and an exhibition of muscle power.

When Mr. Felon's presence was confirmed on the walkie-talkie, a distinctive description was given—short, fair, receding hairline and driving a sports car. More than half the population of my club fell into this category.

And enters, rather exits the third character of this plot.

Mr. Valiant.

The club was shut, the lights glared, the doors were open and people were asked to leave.

One of the many bar patrons who fit the description of the wanted was Mr. Valiant. As he was getting into his red Ferrari with his groupies, he was asked for his identity.

You must be joking.

Mr. Valiant, comes from a family name that's a legacy in this city. His power is legendary and his alcoholism hereditary. And his reverence for law and order very Dilli-like.

Offended and outraged, Mr. Valiant's attempt to snub the confused enforcers of law resulted in an unplanned visit to the cop station in the cop car as a common criminal. The rest of the night was spent in a jail cell sipping black tea.

Why, I had to sign a character certificate, thus taking Mr. Valiant's moral responsibility on my shoulders to get him out of the pen so he wouldn't sue us in the end.

All this while, Mr. Felon remained at large but had to ultimately surrender on a non-bailable deal. With a bit of imagination and muscle power, that could become bailable and who knows who would face the wrath next.

Mr. Bombastic is constantly on probation.

Mr. Valiant is probably still embarrassed because of his infantile behaviour.

Me? Have made another set of friends in Central Bureau of Investigation.

And learnt to be a pushover with these eminent personalities, and let nature take its course.

29

Men on Offer

Oh so this sounds OMG to you? What about 'kept woman' that figures in every other conversation? Trust my luck to find men who want to be kept instead. Where are those happy days when I used to get those offers instead. Why did I decline these propositions without even considering my post-retirement days?

One would think Dilli had a history of chivalry. Gone are the days when you approached the bar counter and a man ordered a drink for you and paid for it too. Nowadays the only time you see a man jumping to offer you a drink as a compliment to you, is at an open bar at a private party hosted by his friend. I guess they are losing their deep pockets because I certainly couldn't have lost my charm.

A few weeks ago, I came across this guy who had relocated to Dilli. We chatted away the night. Upside: he showered all his attention on me. Downside: The drinks were being billed to me. At that time, I didn't care till it came to the point where I was dropping him home.

The next day, out of pure goodwill, I found him an apartment to stay in. He re-payed me by gatecrashing my mother's birthday and looked at me when it was time to go back home. Alarm bells started ringing when he ordered my driver to fetch a pack of cigarettes and assumed the payment would be taken care of by me. This was a one-off thing, I foolishly told myself. Then he came back to my house, drank my Belvedere and told me about the Armani jackets and emerald rings his ex used to buy for him. Then, he fell in love with my guest bedroom and started giving me a redecoration plan that would suit him. All this, considering he was a few years younger to me and was in Dilli as a multinational's contracted employee. Then I was told about all the women in Dilli who were practically throwing themselves at him.

So what was I? A privileged woman singled out by destiny, karma and the Holy Trinity to look after a toy boy.

Well the excuse I used to wriggle out of that one was I had bubonic plague in my armpit.

~

With a relationship status as single, an administrative job and loads of pictures uploaded with my girlfriends, my social network profile is practically an invitation to high-end gigolos offering services that guarantee satisfaction.

One of the inbox messages read (reproduced below *verbatim*. And in case you don't know Latin, that mean 'word for word').

Hi dear,

You look like the kind of person who can benefit from my company as I am sure my company will benefit from you.

Success comes at the price of loneliness. I can take care of that loneliness for a very small price.

I am a good-looking, young, well-spoken and virile man in my early thirties who can offer you total satisfaction. You can check my pictures on my profile.

My list of clients include women like you who are independent and like liaisons with no attachments.

I know how to keep secrets and I am also available for private parties.

My first evening with you will be at no charge and we can work out a financial arrangement for future.

You won't regret making this call. I am available at 98__________.

Love

Tony

Should you want the number, it's all yours.

30

The Light and Lovelies

Light and Lovely

Fact

Highest production and consumption of this face cream in our country
Tried by every third woman in the country at least once
Product available for men, indicating not only gender sensitivity and equality but succeeding in making Indian men as insecure about their complexion as Indian women

Fiction
Permanent effect on the skin as claimed in advertisements

How I know? By using it. How else? The commoner in me couldn't resist the pull of vanity after reading about Snow White as a child. 'Mirror Mirror on the wall, who's the fairest of them all?' The answer is always the exotic white woman from another country.

Capitalising on demand and supply, Dilli is an oasis of Expat Modelling Agencies and Escort Services that address the Dilli Boy's fetish for white skin—uncouth businesses masked with POP (Plaster of Profession) with non-existent employment contracts.

Fair, tall, blonde she must be, with dumb as her USP (a quality that every man secretly desires). An everyday occurrence is our regular Dilli Boy communicating in his unique Haryanvi accent with these lovelies who, in turn, use their rural dialect. The success rate of their relationship baffles the mind. But do I understand it? *Nyet*.

If a Dilli Boy had been present on the fifth day of creation, he would have traded more than just his rib with God to create this ideal mould of his dreams.

But what wasn't a possibility then can be bought by money now.

A very popular boy in Dilli owes his popularity to the arm candies with white frosting. The single-mindedness of his passion makes him wine and dine them (normal), offer accommodation options (weird), lay out a clothing line with unlimited choice (crazy) and throw in a credit line in mid-range stores (psychotic) for a minimum of half a dozen representatives of this cultural assimilation programme worthy of mention in the United Nations. Look pretty and he might take you for all the vacations as well.

Another boy I know of has a package deal going with bulk discount on the purchase of visibility with these girls at all social and bedroom events.

Where to find these light and lovelies?

1. Pool Parties

Pool parties in every hotel or private estate are watering holes these lovelies swarm to every summer. No pool party is complete or successful without their presence or pictures of Indian hairy male arms draped around them.

2. Night Clubs

A pass to the clubbing scene in Dilli with free unlimited drinks is on offer if you walk in with the girlies. The prettier they are, the easier for the queues at the entrance to get cleared faster. No cover charge, no entry charge, only a fully fun-charged night ahead.

3. Vacation at Goa

Oh to walk on the beach hand-in-hand with the bikini-clad lovelies. The pictures of the vacation look spectacular in the end.

4. Indian Weddings

They have the knack of carrying off the tackiest Indian attire, glittery bra-blouses with imitation jewellery, and still be the hottest women in Indian weddings clogged with lacklustre diamond-clad aunties. The *Babes* amongst the Punjabi *Bebes* is essential.

But I salute the patience and thick skin required by the Light and Lovelies to deal with this variety of Dilli Boy. I wouldn't do it for a million bucks...or let's say that's never been offered to me...

31

Worthy, Not so Worthy?

Been through many phases in life and yet so much to see. Am diligently observant.

Call it a sin that can only be compared to indulging in a layered gooey dark chocolate cake when it comes to observing others or call it a curse when it comes to observing my own life, no matter what, I am a brooder.

From my categorisation of people, you can only imagine what I probably do to myself.

In my high-school years, I was a geek, an introvert with self-deprecatory tendencies diminishing my intestines—small and large. Knowing what your problem is half the solution? You must be joking; knowing you have a problem is the beginning of all your issues. Trying to solve the problem, now that's a step forward. Understanding why you are not the most glamorous could help address the issue.

However, in my case there was no enlightenment. Just a snap in the brain, and a gradual change in attitude. Then followed a journey of self-discovery. And in the process,

I discovered a lot more—men, intoxication, self-help books, friends, mentors and all kinds of relationships. I pleased others as I pleased myself.

A few rules I try to follow:

1. You are exactly who you think you are.
2. You are the same person you think everyone else is.
3. You are treated in precisely the same manner you treat yourself when you are alone.
4. You see in others what you choose to see.
5. Others see in you what you decide to show.

I was 21-years-old when I was hosting a post-premiere party of a Hollywood movie launch in Dilli. As an excited manager, I decided to go for a bigger bite of the turnout. One of the guests was an ad-world genius known to be blunt and condescending. Unfortunately, I was not aware of this genial side to him. Passing around some Saki glasses, I came across this man. Over shivering hands, shaking salver, and eventually spilled shots, I promptly offered him some Saki, only to be rebuffed. Now a quick analysis please:

1. I invited him for this party.
2. He was snubbing me for offering him complimentary beverages and personalised service.
3. Just not on.

I treated him just as he deserved and a part of me clearly told him to treat me with respect as I in return snubbed every effort he made now.

Two days later was a blessed Sunday and I was lazing around in my bed when I got a call from this man asking me out for dinner. The desire to unearth his motive won over the impulsive 'No' that almost popped out of my mouth.

Holding open the car door for me at 8 p.m. sharp was this man who guided me inside a gorgeous restaurant. My first question to him was why he had asked me out. He squirmed a little and after a couple of glasses of wine, answered my question—my lovely smile (all crap) and the fact that I was one woman who had been disrespectful to him, thereby challenging his self worth.

So now you know how it works.

32

Heaven and Hell

It's all here... In our Dilli... You can always find heaven in hell and hell in heaven, so neither can be definitively defined.

When you don't find what you need to wear in the evening, it's hell.

When your favourite store displays a sale signage, it's heaven.

When the same dress as yours is worn by another women, it's hell.

When you accidentally spill a glass of red wine on her, it's heaven.

When your ex walks in with another gal, it's hell.

Seeing him being dumped in front of you is heaven.

When you have to wait for a bartender to make eye contact with you, it's hell.

When the same bartender is your old server who remembers your drink, it's heaven.

The glory of every drink inside your tummy is heaven, the bill is always hell. No wonder we always *Pay* for it.

Forget about a single life, all your karmas are levelled out in a single night. For everything else, there is The 'Master's' Report Card.

My perception of heaven and hell is a bit roundabout.

Heaven is a perception of happiness.

God can be found in small things, for example, in a shot glass. Remember, to spread happiness, he converted water into wine.

The monk, Dom Perignon, who dedicated his life to serving others, finally did it by fermenting wine right. Trust me, it helped millions and will continue to do so in the right vintage years.

When you go back home in the early hours, it's heaven. But, as soon as you realise it's morning, it's hell.

When the dreaded alarm rings the siren of torture, it's hell. Every phone call, every meeting, every step towards the conference room for that budget meeting is hell. That slow tick of the clock on your work desk with an inbox of urgent e-mails is hell.

Then the drive back home with the thought of your hot shower, the power nap, the evening's plans—it's heaven.

If hell is a punishment you get later for your sins, heaven is achieved in the duration of that sin.

I have always gained much wisdom during my spiritual hours.

To err is human but how does it matter when it's so much fun. Ergo commit the seven deadly sins, or should

I say, indulge in the seven Dilli Whims, so you don't spend the rest of your life trying to barge into Heaven:

Lust = Libido
Gluttony = Appetite
Greed = Enterprise
Sloth = Stress Management
Wrath = Assertiveness
Envy = Appreciation
Pride = Vanity

33

Dilli With no Boundaries

Two Dilliwalas are entertaining company but more than two is entire Dilli itself. Put us together in any part of the world and we shall recreate a mini Dilli. I, for one, have never been mistaken for anyone other than a Dilliwali, and score as well as the Dilliwala.

Be it four friends on an overnight trip away from Dilli, or four hundred guests for a destination wedding, a group of Dilliwalas travelling outside Dilli will have a kit of premium whiskeys, a hard drive with the latest collection of 'Yo Yo Honey Singh,' portable speakers and at least a couple of efficient men responsible for all of the above.

Now a case study:

Destination: Goa

Occasion: Wedding

Guest list: industrialists, politicians, party-goers and other similar lotus eaters

Statutory warning: All Punjabis

All I can say is *this was a flamboyant wedding*. The italics take care of all the gushing.

The month started with gossip about the choice of airlines, the bulk ticket discount, even the seat numbers. We decided to throw in extra guests and surprise the host.

It was three days of pure madness, with an entourage of assistants at the airport. Our luggage was promptly retrieved from our cars and wheeled in directly for check-in. While we ordered morning coffee, our boarding passes were handed to us. After being whisked through the boarding gate, cars (not buses) transported us to the aircraft. They just stopped short of using designer cranes to takes us from the tarmac to our seats in Club Class. The flight crew must have placed bets on our origins—Jalandhar, Ludhiana, Bhatinda? None of the left. Dilli.

On arrival, Goa received us with finger food and, more importantly, chilled beer right at the airport before we began an hour-long drive to the five-star hotel reserved exclusively for the wedding group.

DJs, *dholwala*s (percussionists) and Sufi singers were all flown in from different parts of the country. Grand set-ups of themes were created to ensure Goa sounded, looked and felt like Dilli with *tangri kebab*s (roasted chicken legs) and Blue Label bottles. If only Dilli had a beach.

The afternoon's scorching sun didn't prevent us from decking up in our heavily embroidered ensemble, with diamonds visible from a kilometre. Neither did the previous night's hangover since the cure was another drink. With a handkerchief in one hand to wipe the beads of sweat (and make-up base) from our foreheads and a chilled beer in another, we danced as though we were in ancient Rome.

As a hotelier, I can easily gauge the magnitude of the rules broken by us—using the hotel pool overnight to multitask; playing loud music at the beach till 7 a.m.; back-slapping the attendants as though they were kindergarten buddies. But the worse may have been trying to stage a Punjabi version of Puccini's *Madama Butterfly* on the lawns.

Another case study:

A friend decided to celebrate his fortieth birthday at a calm boutique resort nestling in the foothills of the Aravallis. Now sane people opt for such destinations for a relaxed, rejuvenating weekend. We clearly didn't have the qualification.

The palatial suites with built-in jacuzzi saw no action since we had got into the theme of 'I am a hunter,' with whips, faux deer and tiger skin, and the works, in the main lawns.

Don't want to go into the embarrassing (for the locals) details but by the time we checked out, the manager must have issued an international red-corner alert for us. The staff looked relieved and delighted to see us drive away.

Call it our trademark, but we Dilliwalas leave no stone, grass and lawn unturned wherever we go.

34

Carpe Diem, Lesbians, Gays, Bisexuals and Transgenders

He was a 30-year-old cool blend of looks, style, education and family background. And a very dear friend of mine. In all honesty, by the time I realised his preference for his own gender, I had rehearsed several ways of declaring my love for him, and getting him to fly away with me to a faraway land on a magic Persian carpet. But the man of my dreams, dreamt of another man. How I cried and cursed my destiny and swore never to fall in love again.

But none of us were at fault. Why should I have read him as single and available, when he was gay?

The man of my dreams took years to come out in the open. The fear of being ridiculed was the most traumatising deterrent. Would his family and friends support him or not? A slow and painful decade of testing waters finally made him plunge into the deep and announce it to the world.

Till date, his family lives in the hope that he will be *cured* while he has finally shed an alien skin to live life by his own rules.

The last I had heard was all that wasn't heterosexual was against the law of nature. Really? Including the earthworm? And who defines what is against nature? The scriptures, worldwide. Ah, those canonical writings that taught us a lot of good but also turned a blind eye to incest, slavery, misogyny, war, murder, loot, plunder, rape, marriages—the list is endless.

So let me say that I have witnessed the joy of loving your own gender and I have seen the sorrow and shame of just coming to terms with it too.

I have danced at gay weddings and also witnessed a gay boy getting married to an unsuspecting girl while his ex-boyfriend was my date for an evening!

I am a regular at gay clubs and the fun is incomparable. The dancing on tables, the hooting and smacking in public, the gorgeously toned bodies with shirts unbuttoned down to the navel—I have spent many enjoyable evenings watching gays doing the salsa. All I can say is that they believe in *carpe diem*—seize the day and live it up.

World-class designers, stylists, writers, artists, professors and tycoons, they have earned the respect of billions. Being a lesbian, gay, bisexual, transgender has never been an issue. Their fearlessness and their work speak for themselves. Awesome listeners, they are also your best critiques, correcting you to perfection.

They know how to shake a leg or two, and have given me some of the best bear hugs I have ever got. In short, some of my best friends are from the LGBT community, and I find it revolting to classify either as criminal or deviant.

The LGBT worldwide are extremely expressive people. Highly intelligent, great conversationalists, compassionate, creative and imaginative, they spin a world in their heads to live in.

Reality is for those who lack imagination, and the LGBT are far from being unimaginative! And to borrow freely from Shaw: 'Must then Christ perish in torment in every age to save those that have no imagination?'

35

Let's Flash

I remember a little game from my childhood: Names, Places, People and Objects. We flash all of these. We love to flash—in our homes, at work, on the streets, while we gym, in shops, at malls and in parties.

You may flash anything. It could be in your driveway, on your body, suspended from your arm, next to you, beneath or above you—from a dead animal flung across your shoulder to the Chihuahua barking snugly in that limited-edition Chanel handbag; an exotic location; an exclusive club; the cards in the wallet and the wallet itself. Let those Italian shoes shine and drop an occasional line on how your style is to add a Canali jacket for an evening out.

Why, the other day at a friend's house, a guy actually came up to me and said we must exchange our visiting cards. Mine was in my Bottega while his was in his car which he quickly amended to his 'Beemer.'

Take care though that it's artfully done and you know how to pronounce the brands you carry. I actually had the privilege of meeting a society lady who complimented another on her excellent collection of *Gukki* and Christian *Dire* bags. With their exterior of monogrammed brand names, let me not go into how YSL is pronounced by some of my closest pals.

Be that as it may, at least one of the following should be said about you in your absence:

> Ah, this guy had the best wheels in town.
>
> Or
>
> We spent last Christmas on his yatch.
>
> Or
>
> Oh my god, she has a fabulous collection of Manolo Blahniks.
>
> Or
>
> They have just bought a lovely house in Kensington Palace Gardens.

If the Dilliwali sports a jewellery store around her neck and wrists, the Dilliwala is conspicuous by the sundial on his wrist (and sometime, the fingers as well).

I once dated a guy with a bigger fetish than me for the brand names. Head to toe, he was always clad in clothes that cost 14 times my monthly income. And he knew everything about the ones I carried—the label, the collection, the season and availability. Basically he knew the price and the value of everything...except me. The only labels I did manage to enjoy that month belonged on the wines.

Now, for the Pandora's Box—from neon-coloured clutches available in Sarojini Nagar to A-grade Louis Vuitton copies from China and Bangkok, half the population tries to pass off the fake for the real.

So flush the flash darlings and reach out for the fig leaf.

36

On A 'Jatt' Plane

I woke up on a regular Sunday with the very clear agenda of doing the household chores carefully listed the previous night, which included detox for that one day (that somehow never works out).

A call from my darling 'Jatt' friend shook me out of my stupor and instead of the usual dose of alcohol pumping in my blood (courtesy the weekend), there was an instant rush of adrenaline, forcing me to pack my bags and get ready in 15 minutes flat.

Yes, you guessed right.

I was off to the airport, with a private jet waiting for me. At that hour though I had no idea where we were headed but honestly who cared?

It was a private jet...

In the car, war-paint was swiftly applied with a hand mirror, alcohol stashed in my bag, glares covering the misdemeanours of the previous night, but somehow I forgot to carry my identification proof for the flight. But who cared?

It was a private jet...

Private terminal, personal security, numerous assistants holding our boarding passes for our convenience, welcomed us.

We were already late for take-off by over 45 minutes, but a specially commissioned personal photographer still managed to click our pictures from three different cameras and light angles for another half an hour with the plane in the background. But who cared?

It was a private jet...

The combination of an eight-seater, a clear view of the cockpit and pilots, a hostess, a security officer was a soothing sight. And beside me was a frightened friend nervously clawing my arms with her nails as we lifted off the ground. But who cared?

It was a private jet...

The morning dose of caffeine missing in the system was compensated by beer with an occasional sprinkling of juice and water. The feast of fried chicken and sandwiches followed, with mouth-watering cupcakes coming up next. Add to that red wine imbibed straight from the bottle. But who cared?

It was a private jet...

The 40-minutes flight was surreal. I was a free bird with clouds at my feet and a huge grin on my face. Glimpses of the fertile greens freshly watered by the monsoons made all of us burst into one patriotic Punjabi song after another although I am not sure we sang in the same octave. But who cared?

It was a private jet…

The descent in a visibly narrow airstrip in Patiala made me pray to the Almighty, which in itself was a very rare occurrence. Climbing down the steps of the aircraft, with my bag in one hand and a bottle of wine in the other, I still couldn't believe my eyes.

It was a private jet…

Patiala is a small city in the heart of Punjab popular for its appetite for liquor. So much so that in India, we have three measures of drinks—small: 30 millilitres; large: 60 millilitres, And *Patiala,* a whopping 90 millilitres. Hence, the carefully chosen destination for the jet ride. Four rowdy Punjabis, we were finally in our element waiting for this one petite, calm and composed girl from the literary state of West Bengal to embrace our culture. Bottoms up on two Patiala pegs did the trick.

Now picture this… a picnic at the airstrip to pay homage to the 'Patiala Peg' with the 'Patiala Peg,' with just a few bushes separating us from the main road where music blared from every passing car and truck. But who cared?

It was a private jet…

When in Patiala, high on Patiala, check into a palace. And that's what we did. An entire floor with private courtyards, backyards and terraces was given to us, with each room approximately the size of my entire Dilli apartment.

As expected, the night unfolded in one of the numerous courtyards at our disposal with...come on, as if you can't guess.

And then in the morning, we were back to the airstrip.

Of course we were late.

Of course we were hung over.

Of course there was a new photo session.

Of course the beer was chilled to the right temperature.

All in a trip of less than 24 hours.

Of course I too am one of those Dilliwalis who lives life emperor size.

But forget that for now, all that mattered was...

It was a private jet...

37

Hitching Up

Heartbreaks come in different shapes and sizes. I had my first one when I was all of 11-years-old. Cold turkey. No response to the hundreds of handwritten cards, the little hearts and trinkets sneaked into his schoolbag. I think I had something to do with this first love of mine changing his school eventually. No, not a stalker. I was just focused and persistent.

Today, if you want to know about my kind of guys—cast, creed, colour, race or age was never a barrier. My excuse? I didn't know what I wanted. And sue me, but I still don't. All I have is sharp outline in my head that lacks the human colours to change it into a work of art. So much for love and longing.

But a friend actually swears by the painful art of tattooing.

It all started long back. To prove his undying, forever variety of love, he had his girlfriend's name tattooed right across his chest. A year and a half later, the girlfriend changed. Seven girlfriends later, half his chest is overrun with strange hieroglyphs. Why, last week he asked me to date him. And I must confess I was sorely tempted to say yes, except the rate at which space was being taken up, he may have tattooed my name around his belly button.

How difficult is it to find the right one? As difficult as a scratch card that promises you the big bumper prize. The coupon is beautiful, your hopes are high and then it ends up revealing a 20 per cent discount on your emotional trauma with the next guy you date, as you know one more thing you need to avoid in future. So all of us poor, single men and women in the city have a handy 'what not to do' list and could start an agony aunt column.

In Dilli's social circles, either the date's reputation precedes him/her or worse, yours. Can't say which is worse. On occasion, your friends, family, (and in some desperate situations, your ex, to atone for having dumped you) finally convince you to meet a match 'made in heaven.' But before that, an entire background check is carried out that would put even the CBI to shame:

1. What car did he come in?
2. How short was her dress?
3. What brands did he wear?
4. What is her family like?
5. What does he do for a living?
6. What does she not do for a living?
7. How much is his family worth?
8. What are her family values?

9. Who does he know in the social circle?
10. Who doesn't she know in the social circle?

Please hide, pretend and act like you were born yesterday. Yes, it includes hiding your age and your true self that you ought only to reveal once there is a ring slipped on your finger.

Hide the real you, create the illusion of what he/she wants in you, ensnare the poor thing into the matrimonial trap so later you can fight till homicide does you apart.

38

For $ale

Show us your money and we might overlook all your... euh...what flaws? In an age of meritocracy, we may even admit your children to a cool school or medical college. Did you say engineering college? Ok, done.

Remember tipping your domestic help as an adolescent to keep your unsupervised adventures under wraps, and the extra tip to the usher for watching that movie in your school uniform?

You are rich, powerful, and absolutely undesirable ('un' is silent).

For you we shall put everything on sale—our time, our affection, our morals, our loyalty, our self-respect.

You might stink from a distance, chew with your mouth open and spit out food particles as you talk. No one complains since you pay a bill of five lakhs at the end of the evening.

You take off your shirt, let the hairy belly protrude, throw champagne on passersby (sometimes along with the bottle) and turn the champagne chiller into a spittoon. But you shall still get the top table at the new club in town, with the manager pleading for your presence when you flash your gold-toothed smile at him.

Your car costs millions, is a technological marvel with a hand-built 4.5 litre V8 engine that produces 582 hp with 398 lb-ft torque. But when you step out of it in your private parking spot at the porch of an expensive hotel, and the liveried staff salute you at the entrance, all we hear is the latest remix of 'Chikni Chameli' blaring from the car. We shall still smile and walk hand-in-hand with you.

You go to listen to one of the world's top five Disk Jockeys visiting the country. His console is at a platform lower than your royal placement from where you look down upon the artist while you eat *rajma chawal* (kidney beans with rice). He will still dedicate his next track to you.

A Michelin-Star restaurant with two stars for their Tuscan specialities books the private dining room for you so that you can order a portion of butter *paneer* (cottage cheese) and *tandoori ghee roti* (clay-oven baked Indian bread with clarified butter). A rare honour for the Maître de.

A meeting is scheduled according to your convenience, you show up 50 minutes late from your gym. Even so, everyone gets up to shake your hand.

You go to Tihar Jail as one of your many scams have been unearthed. Your wife hosts a homecoming bash fit for a king returning after winning a war, to the accolades of well wishers.

For every mistake, there is a bundle of cash. Every tear is wiped away by a piece of jewellery. Every rule is broken with a stick of gold. Every law is challenged with an armour of greenbacks. Money sure is an articulate talker.

Now don't you dare rat on me for saying this, but happiness is now for sale.

39

How Arty Thou?

It's time to defend Dilli and establish it as *the* cultural capital of the country. A lot of other union territories and states might be miffed at being the runner's-up, but Dilliwalas manage to look the part. Warned in time, we can even enact an entire scene at an art exhibition well enough to lift an Emmy.

Yes, there are some serious art aficionados whose knowledge and passion I do not doubt. But then the average Dilliwala is another kettle of fish altogether. The signature on the canvas is always more precious than the work. Investment is what drives us more than an understanding of art itself.

When it comes to owning and displaying art, to each his/her own. At times the same group ends up hanging a dozen impressions of a single work on the walls of the alley leading to the store room or the staircase to the terrace. Why, the artwork on a dear friend's golden-walled and green-marbled mansion was commissioned to a local artist with the brief to recreate a Goya twice the size of the original. In the living room hung cheap Van

Gogh imitations that would have pushed the artist (the Dutch original) over the edge in a way that he would have willingly given away both eyes instead of an ear.

I also have a group of friends who colour coordinate the art they pick up with the toilet seat in the guest room or the broom in the closet, but more of that another time.

On a gorgeous evening, I headed towards an exhibition of art *sculpted* on canvas. Did I mention the theme of the exhibition was 'Yin and Yang in a flower.' This was something I had never witnessed before. With me was my buddy who was a little under the weather, with a phobia of flowers.

The mood in the studio was perfect from the word go. What followed was a mystical experience difficult to couch in language.

The artist was busy explaining why he had used flowers on the large canvas. My friend wilted in front of my eyes while the rest of the crowd oohed and aahhed with every new inflection in the artist's voice. The bold strokes, the great texture, the canvas as an installation, were topics of passionate discussions by a panel headed by yours truly.

Our expert comments must have worn the artist's patience thin for he quickly wrapped up the evening and well, let's say, threw us all out.

At times, an art exhibition doesn't earn the appreciation the artist deserves. What holds our interest is the attendance of the right circles, what they wore, what they drank, how they posed, who they were falling over and what they were tripping on and who said what to whom, why and how. A regular media coverage thankfully carries a brief mention of the artist and the name of the exhibition, while pictures of our Dilli boys and girls are plastered all over Page 3.

The poor artist is an extra in the background unless he is equally flamboyant, with condoms hanging from a Dali-inspired theme, full of what he generously wishes to give back to society. Now that's the kind of debauchery that intrigues us enough to finally unearth that one artistic bone in our body.

Amongst other things, art exhibitions in Dilli are networking hubs. A great Chardonnay with cheese crackers is a fabulous start to an evening that also provides an opportunity to get yourself clicked against the backdrop of modern art looking like unmitigated vandalism. Instead of the artist, it's the poor painting that's been framed for this crime.

Before you draw a blank, consult a good eye. But for all the art that hangs on the walls of my house, and for all the art I cannot decode, every time I see the painting of a naked man, I am tempted to mount it.

40

Lead Us to Light

I am a God-fearing soul but it gets my back up to live in a city that is obsessed not only with character sketches based on the circumstances of birth but the consequences of astrological positions on your future.

My own sister was not allowed to buy new shoes for a year since that would negatively impact the family's fortunes for five years. And if you think I made that up, I can give you her number. I, for one, avoided being seen with her sporting diamonds in her ears and dragging her feet in tattered chappals.

A dear friend has a fatal flaw in her *kundli* (birthchart). She is a *manglik*—any man who marries her would drop dead. The only way out is to get married to a man who is a *manglik* too and who would make her drop dead as well. Now that's what can rightly be called a killer combination, and a great way to start a marriage.

A restaurant's failure is categorically put down to the 'un-vastu' location of restrooms under the sacred *Ficus religiosa*.

Two friends in the same social circle had to get married on the same date as the happy future of their married life depended on it. Juggling two weddings took a greater toll on us than on the fathers of the brides put together. Besides not being able to wear the same dress and shoes to both weddings (just not done)—we had to be present for two *jai mala*s (exchange of garlands), two *saat phera*s (going around the sacred fire seven times), two receptions, two *bidai*s (seeing off the bride). Get the drift?

A big society wedding had the bride decked up in diamonds and rubies the size of rocks—she belongs to a family of jewellers—only to be outshone by her father with precious stones all over his fingers and neck. I wondered if he was hiding sapphire toe-rings as well under his *jooti*s (Indian-style shoes). (And no, the father wasn't cross-dressing as my French friend believed.)

Add to palmists, numerologists and astrologers, new-age self-help gurus who tell you:

1. It's time to say *No* to negativity... Easy, ain't it?
2. If you think your BFF will stab you in the back, she will.
3. If you get sleepless nights worrying your kids will explore drugs, they will.
4. If you believe your wife will cheat on you someday, she will (or worse, she is already doing that).
5. If you consider the possibility of your rival getting that coveted business contract, he will.

6. If you think you'll never find love, you won't.
7. Think positive and all good things will happen.

Well I've tried that too. Clearly doesn't work for salary hikes, annual leave, gratuity, pension, and a few other things.

A few tips on the current crop of new-age gurus who help you regain your balance. They are classified according to the social status and pockets of their devotees.

They live in palatial house called ashrams built on acres of land acquired always by the grace of the Almighty.

They are successful entrepreneurs in the mind-body-spirit industry, with a cool annual turnover of ₹550 crores.

Their dietary suggestions and gymnastics give my personal trainer heartburns.

They offer a single virtual *darshan* for an online payment of ₹3000.

For an additional ₹15,000, they can ensure a soul's journey to heaven.

Discounted rates are available on package deals.

Plans are afoot for Twitter consultations.

They are in talks with a powerful search-engine for a tie-up.

Some venture capitalists are interested in funding them.

Multinational have them on their board of directors.

Some of them have taken over the duties of parents too (barring free *roti, kapda aur makaan*). So you pay to hear the same lectures, albeit accompanied by a benign smile, at a tolerable decibel, and at that time of the day when you are no longer hung over.

Can't speak for the rest of the issues that are *sub judice,* but they certainly don't deter me from wanting to change my profession.

41

It Takes Two to Bango

While a man is gaining experience and growing up (a never-ending process) a woman too does the same, but with a few flattering adjectives: slut, wench, Jezebel, hussy, minx, tramp, strumpet, tart... Hmm.

I understand why we women can't (should be don't *n'est-ce pas* because, we can if we wanted to) piss in public, but why are all *One Night Stands Dos and Don'ts* for men only. A girlfriend has serious issues with the matter and sent me a democratically drawn-up list of Dos and Don'ts for women and One Night Stands:

Dos

1. Go for it only if you want to.
2. You can change your mind anytime. Even Freud gave up trying to figure out why women do that all the time.
3. Blame it on the alcohol, on the prawns cooked with asparagus, on the fatal attraction, on your libido. That helps arguing it out in your head.

4. Tell a friend where you are going and use the safety wrap.
5. Three months down the line, get your head checked.

Don'ts

1. Don't do it because your friends do it.
2. Don't expect anything the next day. If a connection is re-established, it's just a bonus.
3. Don't bring a stranger into your house unless you have someone sharing it (you know the difference between 'it' and 'him') with you. No point discovering an axe and a rope in the boot of his car while you are alone with him.
4. Don't feel like a used rag.
5. Don't blame the man the next morning. Remember, it takes two to bango.

42

Frills Sans Bills

A typical week begins with an accounting of invitations, comparing them with the ones received by your circle and flaunting the ones that give you an edge over them.

I know the top guy of this free 'eat-n-drink' pyramid. He survives on this fare and has earned it through industrious social presence applauded by the social media.

My last credit card statement showed minimum expenditure on entertainment, not leaving much for my tax consultant to account for. It made me think about all the others in this karmic cycle. I am perhaps the smallest fish in the sea, with bigger sharks lined up at the bar. A friend and I counted a record 41 days of not paying the bill while stepping out four days a week... Now look here, all were respectable invitations with constant reminders for our esteemed presence.

My work is to party. I see the same faces, hear the same greetings, indulge in the same small talks, dance to the same tunes, see the same moves.

And I get invited to a friend's *sponsored* birthday, the launch of a new bar or hotel, a fashion-fraternity get-together, embassy dos, a house party or an event or promotion undertaken by a night club (the kinds I manage where I have been specifically asked for complimentary bar as a promotional campaign, and guilty as charged, I have succumbed to this extortion).

My birthday this year was a quiet dinner with ten friends on a Monday evening in an unostentatious, secluded rooftop hangout that can be arrived at after scaling four flights of the most uncomfortable steps. Needless to add, the birthday girl and her invitees were all on eight-inches of heels, making the task rather enjoyable.

A couple whose names I can barely remember decided to join in uninvited. Despite knowing it was my birthday, they didn't offer as much as a simple hug or greeting. Nor were they queasy about trying everything on the menu or being the last ones to leave the intimate gathering, a minute before their bill was slapped on me.

Let me give you an insight of the profit and loss statement of an average Dilli socialite:

Expected expenses

Average minimum cost per night of social frivolities per person: ₹5000

Average number of nights ventured out by the Dilli socialite per week: 3

Expenditure expected per week: ₹15,000

Total nightouts per month: 12

Monthly expenditure per person: ₹60,000

Freebies

Number of free party invites per week: 3
Number of free party invites per month: 12
Total value of free party invites: Rs. 60,000

Add operational cost of hosting a party twice a year. But wait a second, the cost is borne by the marketing budget of a restaurant, bar, hotel and mostly by the liquor company. The bigger the names in your list, the better the spread offered by your sponsors.

To this, one only needs to add miscellaneous expenditure of:

1. Replenishing the wardrobe
2. Fuel and driver
3. Anti-oxidant pills for the morning
4. Intensive quarterly body check-up with emphasis on lungs and liver

Final tally: the cost of living it up in Dilli is minimum, with maximum enjoyment.

43

Post Divorcum

The gift hamper for the man includes:

1. Acute SPTSD—Settlement Payment Trauma Stress Disorder with the unjust division of his assets and forking out the day-to-day living expenses of an ex.
2. Outline on walls left by artworks that once hung there.
3. The empty Ferrari corner that once had six custom-made models.
4. The empty wardrobe where the jewellery locker was kept.
5. The missing limbs of the tree on which money grew.
6. How life made a chopping block out of him.

His true friends remind him that life goes on, that he needs to take each day as it comes, that time is the best healer. They give him the strength to once again regain his strength—for his sake, for his kid's sake and for the future wife's sake.

They take him out to cheer him and eureka...suddenly he realises he is free and has the license to do as he wants even if the license comes at a cost.

A friend underwent the financial whiplash of two divorces but still hasn't lost hope. His second divorce has still not come through and he is already in love with another. His status on social media says, 'Being married is a fact of living. Having a girlfriend along with a wife is the art of living.' So now you know I am not just cooking things in my head.

A woman, on the other hand, goes into a retreat to rediscover the simple pleasures of life—children, family, friends. The homemaker wants to let the storm pass before opening the window to let sunshine and spring in once again.

When she finally decides on making that public appearance, she is applauded and supported. And her reactions are catalogued in the social diary when the ex is around.

Gradually, she too has started revelling in her independence. Kids are taken care of, and for everything else, alimony rules. Now, wanting to enjoy herself as the individual that she is, she purrs into her womanhood. That is, if she hasn't found some spiritual calling in her life.

Then it's time for her to sway her hips again. She vacations, treats herself everyday, throws parties at home.

She makes her own friends without seeking approval of the Lord, God and Master. She is complimented and flattered. And soon she is ready to step into the deceptive web of singledom.

Let me tell you about a friend who has the most transparently spanking clean heart. She was married for almost two decades but her post-trauma self hasn't changed her one bit. You want to talk deception? This one can't even spell that word right. Her opening statement is 'Hi, I am so and so. I got divorced a year back. I have two kids and I am 40-years-old.' She doesn't look a day over 30 but she has this incomprehensible desire to undermine herself lest someone desire her.

Now allow me to talk about a school friend. This is a man in a woman's body. She's been married thrice (I am so jealous as it hasn't happened to me even once). We are the same age for heaven's sake. Despite knowing each other for over 20 years, she never invited me for even one of those three weddings.

And she has made a fortune from all the safes she cleaned out. Way to go. All ye ladies out, are you listening?

44

Photoshop Junkies

I met a woman who claimed to be my friend on Facebook. Not only did I look blank and drunk but totally ignorant and cold when I couldn't recognise her.

When I went home, my guilt did not allow me to go to the bed straight away. Trust me, for I would have hit the bed in my silk-stockings that cost me a bomb ordered online from Macy's, without wiping off my make-up. But no, sitting at my desk, browsing through the lappy, I searched for this woman on Facebook. Fortunately, I remembered her name, for otherwise I wouldn't have found a single similarity between her Facebook profile and the real her.

A beautiful backdrop of blue skies, straight from a movie that won the Golden Globe for special effects, the wind blowing through her hair, making them swirl in the right direction (mine always head in any direction other than what my stylist intended) and a blemish-free complexion that even Kate Winslet would be envious of. She wore an aquamarine dress with a plunging neckline that further accentuated her 40D bust, her 22-inch waistline and her amazingly well-rounded hips, posing in the sand that reminded me of talcum powder. I guess that was the giveaway of the Photoshop.

In another instance, after admiring an acquaintance's beautiful cheeks on her BlackBerry Display Pictures, I decided to go for an acne and anti-scar treatment. And only when my skin was smooth enough did I decide to accept one of her invites, only to offer and suggest the same skin treatment to her.

Photoshop is a great leveller. Black becomes white, white becomes coloured, yellowish become wheatish and brown becomes café au lait.

Photoshop doesn't alter only a person's attributes. My friend Photoshopped his house to make it look bigger, and the grandeur in his updated picture also used in his birthday invite, made me drive past his house twice before I actually recognised it.

That reminded me of the weddings I attended as a child and the fake landscapes in front of which I posed for pictures.

For all we know, the pictures of you petting a tiger in an African safari or a great photograph of you skydiving is all photoshopped. We all know you never went out of town last summer, let alone out of the country on adventure trips.

Yet another acquaintance spends hours altering a group picture so that she looks great and the rest of us look dishevelled, with blotched make-up and in dire need of a dietician and a shrink.

Today, you don't need either the Almighty or the genes of the ones who sired you, or even a doctor specialised in plastic surgery. An updated version of Microsoft and a downloaded programme suffice to make you the person of your dreams. Or try Instagram for instant beauty.

If only mirrors had this option.

45

Page 3, Step-by-Step

1. Future Page 3

A stage when you go to all the social events covered by the leading dailies where you smile and pose at every photographer even if he is trying super hard to ignore your presence. A trip is made to the restroom every 10 minutes to powder your nose just in case the camera showers its attention on you. Or just hover around a somewhat socially known face to embark on your exciting journey in the world of print where you will figure as 'so and so with *a friend*.' At least its a *Friendly* start. If you have ever done this, you are most likely the Future Page 3 and one day will graduate to the next level.

2. Present Page 3

You are the lucky ones featured in all the publications where you claim you don't want to be seen, and are just exploited for your presence in these events. You pretend to shy away from the camera that somehow still captures you in practised poses, showing off your best profile. You accidentally check with the photographer after every click to see that you look gorgeous. Your profession is described as a socialite as it comes naturally to you but hardly do they know the hours spent in front of the mirror to correct the angle of that pearly smile.

Oddly, despite your reluctant appearances, you make that newspaper page your socially visible picture, and tag your entire social group to ensure they can't miss it. A minimum of any two of these attributes make you our Present Page 3.

3. Past Page 3

Recently, a leading daily did an article on the past Page 3 regulars, and published it on Page 3. They were asked what had changed between then and now. Pure venom regurgitated in newsprint made my hand itch; the jealous acidic fumes blurred my vision. Suddenly, the coveted Page 3 had become a paid medium of self-appreciation for the ones who don't deserve to be there. For all those who participated in the defamation vocally, or sulked quietly are the Past Page 3 who can't come to terms with being overruled by the current top dogs.

In short, game over; back to pavilion.

Say what you may, Page 3 is here to stay. All three above-mentioned categories and even those who don't belong there, follow every word of that page relating names to the faces.

When you see unidentifiable pictures of unknown people with captions like 'a party for a special occasion (?) hosted in a bar (?) saw some people (?),' rest assured no money has exchanged hands or else at least one name would have been mentioned.

Don't worry. Brilliant offers and discounts make it easier to shop for fame. These ensure brand visibility and social promotion, especially if you use your company's name as your last name even if it's a brand for cat food.

A few years ago, I would see half a dozen same faces once a week and wonder what they did that the others didn't. Well, they enrolled in a social appreciation programme called Page 3.

How it works

It is a one-time opportunity—a monthly or an annual package—that guarantees a minimum number of appearances but if you are friends with the reporter, you can get a few free add-ons.

Next, all you have to do is make all required appearances, walk into the party stalked by the photographer as you sail through, hugging everyone (even the ones you don't know) for that perfect picture to be used for both the virtual and print media.

And since practice makes perfect, to fulfill your ambition of being a socialite and, a household name in Dilli, just be a social zombie—in your head, and watch the results—in print and on self.

46

Parentology

This couple provides equilibrium in my life, in the merry-go-round world I live in.

Randomly introduced to them at 1 a.m. amidst loud music, I barely even registered their names. But as fate would have it, two hours later, they were in my house. One of them pretended to cook (not one of her strong suits), the other actually making a fine fist of my bar, pouring everyone XXL drinks.

Everyone drifted along till an alarm for 7 a.m. rang in our paradise.

Their seven-year-old daughter had her school bus coming at 7:30 a.m. In twenty minutes flat, round, square, they were at home in *Noida*. Mommy had to kiss her cheek and daddy had to drive her to the bus stand. This morning custom was not up for debate, the late-night revelry notwithstanding, except that day, Daddy was chewing on mint to mask the smell of whiskey and mommy couldn't walk straight in her heels with running make-up camouflaged by dark glasses.

It's called management skills. Be the first one your child sees in the morning, and the last one before she is put to bed with an additional few hours between school and ballet classes.

Teach her the new poses for photo-ops, dress her up with jewellery and make-up. It's the one thing this life-size doll lives her day for.

And when I ask this two-foot bundle of joy what she wants to be when she grows up, she says, 'I wanna grow up to be mama, get ready, wear new clothes and go party.'

Another mom is a style icon of this city and has featured on the covers of top magazines. She diligently wakes up in the morning to drive her daughter to the kindergarten, tuition classes, correcting her grammar when the little one asks for 'The Papa,' catching her forty winks in between so she is peachy again to step out in the evening in her new high heels to shake a leg to 'I'm Sexy And I Know It.'

Just as I think this can't get more interesting, I enter the room of another friend's four-year-old son. He has aligned all his super hero action figures and says *cheers* and *salut* with his glass of milk to each one of them.

Then there are moms who instill the belief of rough-cut diamonds in their children. Yet others shape them up in adolescence. A nine-year-old daughter is physically shaped by the food served to her; mom and daughter jog together in the backyard (even if this mom has a hairline fracture); there is a mini gym in the child's playroom and a genuine look of excitement on the mom's face when the nanny informs her that her child missed a meal. And don't you dare chew the mom over for this; I wish mine had treated me this way. This one child is the most poised nine-year-old you shall ever meet, and who can have an intelligent woman-to-woman conversation with you. Every time I go to their house, I feel I have two girlfriends instead of one. Her knowledge on fashion is commendable and her style tips come straight out of *Harper's Bazaar*. If Suri Cruise has her own fashion line, its most important client would be my friend's kids.

So here's the new alphabet for these alpha kids:

A for Alexander McQueen
B for Balenciaga
C for Chopard
D for Dolce and Gabbana
E for Elie Saab
F for Fendi
G for Givenchy
H for Hermès
I for Issey Miyake
J for Jaguar
K for Kenneth Cole
L for Louis Vuitton
M for Maserati
N for Nina Ricci

O for Omega
P for Prada
Q for Quintessentially Membership
R for Rolex
S for Stella McCartney
T for TAG Heuer
U for Ulysse Nardin
V for Valentino
W for William Tempest
X for X Box
Y for Yves Saint Laurent
Z for Zegna

And honest to God, sometimes these kids pronounce the brands names better than the parents.

Their birthday parties are no less than any social event in your calendar, and marked a month in advance. At party supplies stores, authentic Disney products are hand-picked by the children. With themes like 'Disco Deewane,' the clothes are made in designer workshops for everyone invited, including grown-ups like me. Professional photographers are hired and every year's party album is as thick as the parents' wedding albums. Sometimes the photographs are also splashed on Page 3.

A spring carnival birthday has us jumping on bounces, ordered especially keeping our age in mind.

But once the kids tire out, the dance competition is now between us adults. A party that started at 4 p.m. continues till 4 a.m.

And then the alarm rings for 7 a.m.

No expense was spared in a Formula 1 theme party where a mini track was created in the lawns to race the super car models especially imported for the occasion and a $250 car given to each child as a return gift.

After this party though, I was deeply disappointment when I went for a 14-year-old's birthday at the riding club and didn't come back home with a pony. But I did manage the phone numbers of some good-looking horsemen with great riding skills.

47

In Debt We Shall Rise...

...From the ashes of the Phoenix Bank of India. A penny borrowed is a penny earned. If you ever want to get rid of someone, lend him that penny and wait for the magic.

A wise man once said, 'If you want to know what God thinks about money, just look at the people He gives it to.' And for the have-nots, Dilli is the loan-some capital that lends money to people to buy things they don't need—cars, homes, businesses, vacations, life.

Maxed-out cards to 'bill to company' agreements for lifestyle enhancements are time-tested methods of cashless transactions. On occasion, you may lose the friends you borrow from but you stand to gain another set of flies with the honey you buy from someone else's dosh.

A friend from Dilli was desperately pulling strings to meet the head of the corporate loan division of one of the leading multinational banks. Somehow I got the whiff of it. Hence, imagine my surprise when I bumped into him at The Box in London, hosting a table worth £20,000 on his personal expense. He was all smiles as though ready to celebrate another scam successfully pulled off by his company whereby he believed the loaned money belonged to him. He had once proudly declared, 'We take it, our books absorb it until it finally disappears and then everyone else pays for it.'

Unfortunately a scam was unearthed, a jail sentence of a year for fraud was awarded and served. And lo and behold, he emerged from the prison gates smiling as though he had won the elections, stepped into his Lamborghini in quest of the next sucker who would give him ₹200 crores, with more loved ones cheering the motorcade.

I see the likes of them day in and night out. Their signature style includes suites booked in seven star hotels, parties hosted with caviar, family weddings running up expenses that could fund seven generations of education at Eton and Harvard, and an uninterrupted good life till the next Financial Review Meeting with the lender.

Financial rules of Delhi

1. Spend more than you earn. Your gross habits must be more than your net income.
2. Neighbour's envy is lender's pride but make sure no one knows about it.
3. The art is not in making money but in making up money.
4. Money can buy you love, looks and all the happiness in the world.
5. You may suffer from depression but not recession.

6. Opposites may attract, but with similar bank balance.
7. Sow a financial façade if you want to reap social blessings.
8. A wise man has more money in his head than in his locker.

48

And the Road Rage Winner Is...

Let's say, you are driving a Bentley, Aston Martin, Bugatti, Rolls Royce, Jaguar, Lamborghini, Ferrari, Audi, BMW, Mercedes or any other car worthy of mention here that I would have skipped. Yes, we can afford them, and yes, we have all of them, or at least one of the above.

Irrespective, you have to roll down your window and scream at the driver in the car beside yours, championed by other drivers in the jam cheering you on with their horns.

We are world champions in driving etiquette or at least that's where we are headed. In a right-hand drive country such as ours, each one of us has overtaken from the left, changed lanes at least ten times in the course of five kilometres, skipped a red light, accidentally grazed a car in the parking lot and sneaked out, taken a wrong way in a one-way street, driven on the pavement in desperation, overshot the speed limit, disregarded the seat-belt rule, entered a no-entry zone, zoomed across a zebra crossing, and honked in silent zones.

Everyone in this city is a stunt driver, pulling unexpected stunts at every corner. Yet, the moral indignation that makes you break into a righteous frown when somebody does it in front of you is amusing. And, if it has a direct impact on you, the 'Beautiful Beast' kicks in. A verbal volley is complemented by *mudras* and other equally elegant gestures. Soon you resemble your earliest forefathers and lunge at the opponent before a war is declared.

All this has to happen on some of the busiest intersection in the city, especially when there's a flight to catch or the most important meeting of the year is lined up ahead.

Within seconds, your driver follows in your footsteps. My proud friends narrate how their drivers and personal security officers handle the situation by man-handling pedestrians, competing with other drivers, and believe it or not, with the authorities as well.

I learned how to drive when I turned 18. My own road rage was such that my father politely recommended a driver and I heed that piece of wisdom to this day.

Let's get to the bottom of this bravado we are renowned for in the country.

I list below the revered teachings of an experienced mentor:

1. No matter whose fault it is, you are always right. Jump for your right and fight the fight. Whoever wins gets paid for the damages.

2. Intimidate the cops. The bolder, the more confident, the more aggressive you are, the better your chances of getting away with your breath reeking of booze, an expired insurance or, better still, no license.

3. Be the one with staying power. If you venture into this terrain, you must fight till victory and the laurel wreath, both have been acquired justly or through a combination of lungpower, fisticuffs, uppercuts and kicks in the groin.

Anyone intruded into your territory (Dilli's road fall in that category), must pay. And if that still doesn't calm you down, never mind, just run into another car, or over a few people resting on a sidewalk.

49

The Philosopher, Guide, Mentor

Don't humour them. Avoid them. And never ever give in to them. Feel free to slap them if things get out of hand.

I know a sample, not so easy on the eyes, in the age group of 50-70 years, an averagely loaded skunk, closely connected with the political class. His CV is a mile long and he even comes with his own website, with a string of achievements no one else seems to know much about. And he sure knows his vowels, mainly the 'Oohs!' and 'Aahs!'

In one of Dilli's evenings, this sugar daddy started chatting with me rather matter-of-factly. He insisted I was in the wrong profession and could do much better. With the benefit of hindsight, I realised he was referring to the oldest profession practised by a woman.

Once, however, I did give into the temptation of attending one of his social networking parties in a seven star hotel suite. Conservatively dressed, I walked into a hall full of powerful rich SOBs waited upon by some of Dilli's top socialites throwing themselves all over politicians and other worthies, for benefits that ranged from personal goodies to that business deal for an already rich husband who wanted to be even richer.

Hands roved around knees, shoulders pressed against the couch, bosoms strained against corsets, and key cards to rooms did more rounds of the suite than the drinks.

A speedy exit with polite but quick byes still didn't help. For months on end, every time I bumped into one of those rakes, he would not believe that I was unavailable. What's more, each time I ran into one of those ladies, I invariably ended up getting that 'I know what you did the last four seasons' look.

Dilli can be quicksand for young girls, and abounds in the voluntary offering-of-the-self by the not so young 'respectable' Dilliwalas.

Dumas, my absolute favourite, had said, 'All human wisdom is contained in these two words—wait and hope.' Waiting and hoping like hell for the masks to fall soon.

50

Botox Queen

Don't smile. It might wrinkle your face.

It's time to burn the padded bras and spandex, wipe away the blotchy make-up, peel off the fake eyelashes and pull out those hair extensions. Life offers you everything at the swipe of your credit card. Money can't buy you happiness (actually it can, refer above) but it can buy you plastic surgery which comes close enough.

I, for one, believe my nose resembles that of a teddy bear. But according to Dilli's leading dailies, it's a carefully strategised upturned nose straight out of a magazine. Thank you, imaginary plastic surgeon and real God. No point denying what my enlightened friends think is true. Nothing can stop them from being nosey about my nose. Moreover, I take it as a compliment for my *Natural* nose.

No face-lifts, no liposuction, no breast implants. The mere mention of such things is offensive. Everyone denies it with the same vehemence that I just did because we are all natural beauties. Don't be fooled by the stony reaction to such suggestions—it's just a side effect of scalp stapling.

The Dilli diva is always God's creation and not the doctor's. Plastic and cosmetic surgery are terms of the past. Today is the day of 'aesthetic' surgery, which makes 'your inner beauty reflect on the outside.' This means our Vedic sages are out of jobs. This also means your 'inner beauty' is directly proportionate to the depth of your pockets. This inner beauty isn't a birthright of the fairer sex anymore. Men need to realise their inner beauty too.

The menu offers you a choice of rhinoplasty, body contouring, facial cosmetic surgery, fillers, lasers and more.

From hair transplant to liposuction or paunch reduction, surgery is a must and thankfully so. My college sweetheart developed large moobs (male boobs) and gave me a run for my money. Trust me, that's the last thing you ever want to compete for with your man.

However, do be mindful of the following once you wear your inner beauty on more than just your sleeve:

Since most of you would be non bio-degradable and non-recyclable, you would pose an environmental hazard with your silicon footprint.

If cloning ever becomes a reality, your clone from your DNA may not look like you.

Acting, enacting or reacting to anything may become impossible. The only emotion shall be the one the doctor literally etched on your forehead. Permanently raised eyebrows, shock, indifference, mild surprise or permanent fright are the currently available facial options. And you can choose only one.

If you ever had a twin lost in our famous Kumbh Mela, the biggest ever carnival, you shall never be able to reunite with that sibling.

You can never say you got your good looks from your mother.

Now the pluses.

You can finally have people kissing your ass once you transport the fat from buttocks to your lips.

You can bequeath your breasts to your daughter in your will.

Even if you are unemployed, the nose will always have a job (ok, not so funny).

On a boring date, you can always blame Botox for your expression.

You can finally do some community service. In your absence, your friends can tell their kids, 'Beta, eat your greens or Botox auntie will come.'

All said and done, I champion the Botox Queen as in a few years, I am sure I will be walking with fillers in me. Only, I would love to show it off to all and pioneer an international craze for Botox Kitty Parties. Botox Kitty Parties would be the next concept that I would like to patent.

Jokes aside, before going for the Botox, think long and hard. The toss-up is between looking your age and looking your species.

51

From Columbia, With Love

The three Cs of life cracked: Coca Cola; cocaine; coffee in the morning.

For some godforsaken reason, I see snorting noses everywhere I go. It's that thing straight from Columbia. Fortunately, for many, nobody's watching or else they'd be snorting for a different reason.

A snorter I happen to know, has been stuck in the groove for over 15 months now: 'This is the third time in my entire life. I never do it otherwise.'

Charles (as it's popularly known as) makes you love life, focus on the biggest intoxicant of them all—you and yourself and the complete package including the latest nail art and Louis Vuitton thongs. The energy rush makes life all good and solves every problem dating from 326 BC. You do it at home, in bars, at private parties, behind the sofa, under the futon. I mean snort, if I sounded equivocal.

A friend's friend tries it, encourages the friend who encourages another friend—thus is the direct marketing chain set up. It's fun, it's cool. It's trendy and endorsed by the rich and famous. If you snort, you have arrived. For midnight cravings, phone a friend. And if you have it on you, consume straight from the packet, then blast off to heaven.

At a private party, a social brat barely in his twenties was using his lung power to draw attention to his need for it. A friend and I wanted to see if he wanted the high of a drug or just the high of doing a drug. So purely for the sake of research, we offered him Alprax. Not only could he not understand the difference but he bounced about the lawns high on a substance that ought to have put him to sleep.

These vacuum cleaners also are pathological liars, hiding their stash and begging others for their next fix. Or lying to the loved ones and doing it on the sly.

There is nothing happy about this happy drug. But by the time you realise this, the mental and physical wear and tear has already set in. The 'snow' that you inhaled with your nostrils wide open now snowballs into a disaster.

The upside—you'll stay skinny 'coz you just won't eat. So, this one is from the immediate circle of my friends. A friend is desperately trying to loose those stubborn extra pounds. A few weeks back, she came to my house after her weekly meeting with her dietician. Sad, dejected and separated from food, the poor girl was crestfallen at the diet suggested to her. A few drinks down, we Googled *How to lose weight without exercise or diet control.* Yes! The answer was cocaine!

Cocaine vs Carbs

1. Cocaine is easier to use and can be consumed straight from the packet.
2. Cocaine recipes require no special cooking skills.
3. Cocaine burns your body whereas you need to plan how to burn carbs the next morning.
4. Cocaine midnight cravings are easier to satisfy with a call to an understanding friend.
5. Cocaine revs up life while carbs slow it down.

So go for it. You'll look great while you are alive and then you'll join your understanding friends in afterlife.

52

VIP

One day I got a call from a guy asking me out on a date. He had VIP passes to listen to some soulful Sufi music at a *dargah*. I couldn't miss this one for the world—VIP access to Allah himself.

Vaishno Devi, Shirdi and Tirupathi, like many other places of worship in India, too recognise you as a Very Important Person *for the right amount*. I'll be honoured if I was considered just a flea in the eyes of my creator. We had always been told we are the children of God and equal in his eyes. But to be a VIP in his house of worship? My life's goal can now be offered to me on a platter.

Cut to Dilli where everyone is a VIP, a Very Important Person. The term is used for *homo sapiens* and for passes for matches, zones in concerts, access to nightclubs, private rooms, front rows in fashion shows and award ceremonies, seating in plays or movie screening, parking area spots. You name it, and everything is qualified as VIP.

Clever ploy. Step up the demand and quadruple the price—the business sutra behind the VIP treatment.

But who exactly is a VIP?

A very important person acknowledged by other VIPS.

A very important person invited to events by other VIPS.

A very important person seen only with other VIPS.

We are talking about the cherry picks of the Dilli Chéris.

Now I just wonder how special is this feeling when half the social circle in Dilli falls in the category of VIP.

Or a Very…

Idiotic Person

Impossible Person

Immoral Person

Incorrigible Person

Immodest Person

Impatient Person

Insane Person

Insulting Person

Irritating Person

Well, pretty much an all-rounder.

53

Dilli Police

I am not debating their effectiveness or lack thereof. But they sure are *with you, for you, always.*

We decided to celebrate a girlfriend's birthday in a hired limousine. If there is a rule prohibiting drinking in a limousine parked in a public place, we were blissfully unaware of it as the chauffeur, by now trained to be deaf, dumb and blind, drove us through and around Chanakyapuri and India Gate, both high-security zones. Not once were we stopped; instead barricades were pulled aside for us. And when an occasional torch was shone inside, they took up our offer to join in the celebrations... for a modest fee of a few hundred rupees.

How cool are they...

With you, for you, always.

Everyday, drunk drivers in expensive cars are let past checkposts for a mutually agreeable fee, a unilaterally demanded case of Classic Mild, and a freshly opened bottle of Old Monk (that is just the 'front' drink). All this, while chit chatting across a rolled-down window of a

Mercedes Benz Sports Tourer. No wonder we feel safe on the Dilli roads.

They too party every Saturday.

With you, for you, always.

A house party with loud music is generally a gold mine. A farmhouse or a wedding party, and local cops queue up in the driveway faster than you can dial 100. The deal is usually struck beforehand and when the party is in full swing, a self-righteous team of law-keepers walk in and hang around till it's time for them to titter out after a few drinks, a bellyful of food and of course the moolah.

They join in the celebrations.

With you, for you, always.

Every business, especially those involving late-night operations, alcohol or entertainment, needs to serve up a monthly package over and above the daily tip. In our lingo, these referred to as the Officer's Kids Education Fund.

'Police and Sons Limited' runs it...

With you, for you, always.

If you are from an influential Dilli family, and caught erring on the wrong side of law, you are innocent until proven *innocent*. But innocence is directly proportionate to diminishing influence. Or let me put it this way, we are all equal in the eyes of law till some schmuck comes up with a contact—an uncle in politics, a senior official who is daddy's friend, an official familiar with your track record of generosity.

A friend filed a fraud case committed against his company. Despite constant follow-ups, the case file and the string tied around it gathered dust, and more dust. But the minute a contact was pulled out of the hat, my friend was called to the right office, offered lunch where his preferred Chinese cuisine was served in initialed steel plates of the department. Two phone calls, two days and two culprits were in custody. Bravo.

They promote healthy socio-economic disparity.

With you, for you, always.

So we have a very lucrative industry of *liasoning* professionals and dealmakers—those who know the right people who would help achieve the right results and steer everything in the right direction. Millions are traded and earned with this network and people are increasingly taking to it as an entrepreneurial venture.

Gone are the days when people flaunted their contacts for social climbing. Now, it's a serious money-making mechanism that thrives on those who need to break the law and those who are meant to enforce law. Learn to look at the larger picture—Dilli Police generates innumerable opportunities for an alternative profession…

With you, for you, always.

And if them cops think they can now put me on their hit-list, I have a few contacts too.

54

The Forties Gang

Like a pod of whales, they form a social group, and always go out together for a spin, to hunt their prey, or on a holiday. The bond goes beyond the 'mother and calf' bit to mutual mothering and smothering.

This particular group consists of the rare species of Killer Whales—highly social, sophisticated, epitomising culture passed down generations.

And luck is on their side. They are neither threatened nor endangered. Found in the usual haunts of hi-end Dilli malls and boutiques, they bulk-buy the same style of bags and shades, with brand names screaming out loud.

Recently, at a popular optical store in Khan Market, a new model of sunglasses was named after one such person because she led the pod that bought them all.

For the forties gang, a typical day is spent indulging in four prime age-reversing activities: foraging, resting, travelling and socialising. Decked from head to toe in the latest fashion money can buy, they resemble clones of different colours. Their blow-dried hair, with blond tints (comes at no expenses, if the hair drier is mercilessly used everyday) helps in head counting as they traipse into the closest restaurant after a day of toil at Emporio. Tons of flesh top swollen feet stuffed into dainty stilettos. A predictable order of raw fish (expected diet) in the form of sushi is washed down with a few glasses of wine, while each one asks for an extra chair or stool to put down the result of their day's work—shopping bags of all shapes, sizes and colours.

The discussion centres on very serious topics of national interest—domestic help turnover, the next big occasion, venues for parties, choice of party planners, the dress for the evening, the upcoming wedding season, common vacations, unreasonable demands made by in-laws including the wish to speak to you for a minute a day.

Rarely does this discussion veer towards concerns about their children's grades. Instead, they beam with pride when their cute little ones publically display their understanding of luxury brands, their new boyfriends and girlfriends, and their own set of parties.

Occasionally, the forties gang takes along teenage daughters as well for an early introduction to Dilli's who's who. For the lack of finishing schools in the city, techniques of the social graces such as hypocrisy are handed down from mother to daughter.

Colour coordination is way too down market for them. Today it's all about 'gen-coordination'—the mother-daughter duo wearing the same style by the same designer, sporting the same haircut by the same stylist and even ordering the same cuisine from the same server. It's the current hot trend making you wonder who's trying to compete with whom. And don't be surprised if the forties gang wants to be crowned the winner.

It's only once they sit in their respective chauffeur-driven cars after a social afternoon that behind-the-scenes gossip begins—who wore what; who was seeing who; who didn't have a designer bag; who repeated those fake Louboutins; how Kate Middleton, a commoner, had delivered the third in line to the British throne.

The afternoon's experience is re-enacted for the ones who 'just don't know what they missed.'

Yes, the forties gang may be flawed. But putting aside their carefully concealed disdain for each other, they are all achievers—at the click of their pencil heels, the Dilli men married to them follow without a whine.

Way to go blubbers.

55

Facebook Friends in Dilli

I have over 2000 friends in my account but really do end up interacting with 20. The others are there for the mutual need to be in each other's life, in case you can benefit from their position, situation and claim to fame. They also help you to increase the number of friends, followers and eventually the 'likes' on your status updates and the pictures posted.

No matter how confident we are of our place in the sun, we need to see how many out there pine for us. Every comment and 'like' makes us feel important. Clearly a high-school level entertainment.

The relationship status changes regularly, owing to a tiny fight as the world is invited to watch the mud-slinging, and possibly applaud.

Self-proclaimed food critics with zilch qualification in the field, trash competition to promote a restaurant in the vicinity belonging to a friend.

Political maestros back a corrupt government or feign offense at a political remark. With hidden agendas, they use Twitter and Facebook as relationship-building tools, with a dagger in the cloak for virtual political assassination.

The music buff is glued to the speakers in a bid to impose on others less evolved, the art of music appreciation. Those desperate to look cool, upload electronic dance music while secretly loving Air Supply (however uncool, it is still my favourite band).

Then there is *Fikipedia*—when Facebook is treated as an encyclopaedia. The questions range from where to eat, pray and love; which hairstylist to visit for that life-changing cut; which is the coolest nail art hangout; what would be a better holiday destination than Ibiza; who has eloped with the neighbour's cat...

And let's not forget gaming. With all controls at your fingertips, you can be fast and furious, and all impossible missions can be accomplished. You can create your world and destroy others. The spirit of competition is instilled. A winner is born. You are the master of your fate, your destiny.

Facebook also comes in handy when you wish to wash your dirty linen in public. With one comment, you could be pissing all over the *Wall*. The guilty ones defend and the offended ones berate.

What I like is the harmless fun and anecdotes. So here's some gratis advice for you:

Use a profile picture that is Photoshopped or better still, clicked by a professional for a measly fee of ₹20,000.

Add friends even if you don't know them because of their mutual friends with the right networking.

Have a dog-adoption link or save-a-child flashing, even if you don't contribute a penny.

Secretly check profiles of your ex's, and rejoice if they have become fat and ugly.

Post all the picture you took with those Bollywood stars who looked the other way while you insisted on glueing yourself to their side.

Display your latest picks: babes, dudes, watches, yachts, palaces, private islands.

The latest trending tool—make a page for yourself: Srishti Khanna—designer, painter, writer, healer, shrink, stylist, lifestyle critic, sarcasm expert, shoe-shiner, ass-wiper, etc., and get as many likes as possible.

Or, if you insist on being lacklustre…update your status with the daily temperature, humidity levels and rainfall.

And if you know you have limited social skills, you might want to outsource your personal account to a professional.

A bargain queen with a shrill voice, with unlimited means but limited grey matter has contracted her Facebook account to her photographer. The pictures, the updates, the love for children and appreciation for her husband (who's actually paying the bill) is all done by this paid butter dish but the fact that he tags himself on his client's wall to say, 'Oh thanks darling for making me look so beautiful in your pictures' is maybe a little weird. What say you?

56

Bolly-Hooked

The entire country is sold on the movie industry including our very own Dilli. Top bureaucrats, business houses, fashion designers and us commoners are completely 'Bolly-Hooked.'

Just send the press a list of people (even an unheard of small-screen actor shall do) 'from Mumbai,' and see the flashlights at work. From top journalists to a million bloggers, all scramble for a few minutes with these stars 'from Mumbai.'

Our local queen throws parties for these visiting dignitaries. An entire week goes into planning—broadcasting the impending visit to everyone you know, hoping it shall travel farther afield; picking up the star (?) from the airport (if not already flown to Dilli in your private jet); getting hotel bookings done or rearranging your master suite for the GiG (Guest-is-God). And more importantly, devising ways to flaunt the 'family member'—shopping at your friend's designer store, especially when he's around; booking the centre table in the busiest coffee shop in town so the world can see who you are with and an unannounced visit to your salon to file your accidentally chipped small toenail. Then comes the evening party.

Every guest from Mumbai is flown in for a purpose—promoting a 'cause' funded by the company's expense sheet booked under advance losses for image gain: fashion shows with a one-movie actor who as an action hero looks resplendent in a velvet '*churidar*'; an item song dancer of the '80s gyrating at a wedding; the current movie diva opening a holistic hospital wing; a club's opening night with a star appearing for no more than 15 minutes.

I have had the fortune of being associated with the best lifestyle food and beverage places, and on one particular occasion, was directly interacting with the loveliest, breathtaking and a super successful 'God of Social Gods.' His regular presence in Dilli for a movie shoot ensured my best nightclub profits for those two months. Till date, everyone wants to know what he is all about in person, which is acceptable. What is not acceptable is regular calls from unknown numbers on my personal mobile phone at 3 a.m. to find out if he is in town and where they can see him. Two calls on an average a day are about his contact details.

Another truly 'Bolly-Hooked' friend is a designer with a store where Chandni Chowk meets Swarovski. The guy now demands money to go to public events, so he can pay for the trips of the ones sashaying down the ramp in his shows, and courtesy whom he became a local celebrity.

I too have quite enjoyed their presence and attention, from the time when I was introduced to a superstar on a first-name basis, to the famous pose struck for me by the lead of a National Award-winning movie, and the song whispered in my ear by the voice whose CD blares in my car. And I proudly narrate these encounters in every possible social scenario.

You would probably expect small town folks to be star-struck but if you see the zoomed-in shots of 'partying with the stars,' you would realise this love knows no boundaries, no class distinction, no bank balance and absolutely no public humiliation. We all queue up screaming their names, just for a handshake, an autograph, or a picture with them for the family album.

Hook(ed), line and sinker, I attended the wedding of the only son of a well-established Dilli family. The theme was Filmfare Awards.

The best emcees in the industry enacted to perfection their love for the family shelling out the crores. Every aunt and uncle's name was taken as though they were guests at the White House. With seating for a thousand guests facing the stage, it was a packed show with back-to-back performances on the most popular songs by A-grade actors that could put any award ceremony in the shade.

Only when the show was over did we realise that we were at a wedding. So, while the order of each performance is forever embedded in my mind, I still cannot recall the groom and his pretty bride's names.

57

Can I Be Your Canine?

It's raining cats and dogs in Dilli. The otherwise stone-hearted Dilliwalla now goes over the top with love for animals. You have to understand, whatever we do, we do it with a swagger or we don't do it at all.

Doggies or kitties, as they are now referred to, are a must in every household socially worth citing. But none of those white furry Pomeranians of the '90s puhleez. They are clearly middle-class today.

And do not commit the cardinal sin of being seen with a breed similar to the one of The Joneses. Go to great lengths to find that one pedigree that makes everyone wonder if it even belongs to this planet. Great Danes, Saint Bernards, Chihuahuas and Persian cats are the flavour of this decade. Either they need to fit the largest room in your house or the smallest bag in your wardrobe.

Jog with your high breed and judge others by the breed that pants by their sides. After all, if your pooch can help expand your social circle, where's the harm?

Walk the ramp with your dog. If you don't have the looks, the dog will make up for it.

Gatecrash a party by landing up with your dog. Ignore the huge *'No Dogs Allowed,'* and walk right in, pretending to be an animal activist.

Once I went for a 'bring your own dog' party with my Labrador who is loveable to boot and dumb as they come. To forewarn people of his attributes, his name is Bonkers. His leash was taken from me at the entrance of the host's mansion, while comfortably sneeked into the parlour with a glass of champagne. All seemed well till Bonkers refused to follow the directions of the instructor and during the obstacle course, when warned of the hump ahead, he (Bonkers, of course) chose to focus only on the word 'hump.'

I am not too sure how many junior Bonkers he sired that afternoon but I know that my friends never forgave me his lack of etiquette. Be that as it may, I proudly claim my dog is a happy soul. But I do feel like beating up people who confine the loudest, largest and highly spirited pets to a two-bedroom apartment. All for social acceptance.

Alternatively, adopt a stray who despite of your great proclamation of love, shall loiter outside your gates. Get it vaccinated, neutered and de-wormed. And feed it sporadically. That should settle a few issues with the soul, and if you can embroider reality a bit, your story about that dog could even be sold to a filmmaker.

In an era when you flaunt not only your physician, dentist, shrink, plastic surgeon, your chauffeur's designer clothes, don't forget to flaunt your vet. And remember to add that your pet sleeps on Persian silk in an air-conditioned room with heavenly aroma wafting from designer burners; is trained by the best trainers in the most expensive pet schools; visits the salon twice a month; is well tended by an entire regiment of beauticians who gladly come home to ensure only butter-soft paws ever touch you; wears Ralph Lauren summer clothes made from the same high thread count cotton the designer uses for your shirt.

I am no animal and I have spent most my life trying not to be a pet. But I really wouldn't mind if someone send me to a spa with a diamond dog collar.

58

Insomnia Buddies

From dusk to dawn,
An insomnia buddy is born.

And a fatal attraction binds us in a formidable bond. Ergo, you have a dependable group for entertainment post 1 a.m. each night, including weekday nights.

Last summer, my friend was visiting me for a week. The idea was to ensure she partied every night of that week. With the nights progressing as Dilli nights do, soon it was a depressing Tuesday. Underestimating my insomnia buddies, my friend thought planning a party at 9 p.m. on such a dull night was a futile idea.

At 1 a.m., we were still sitting alone in my house with a bottle of wine for company. And then it happened.

The doorbell rang.

And rang.

And rang.

An army of my insomnia buddies stormed into my house, raided more than the pantry, fired the music and we all had a blast. That night my parents decided to leave my name out of their wills.

To make a success of these impromptu bashes every night, the insomnia buddies have to ensure a few things:

1. A place to party without grumpy parents or neighbours
2. Emergency alcohol with a 24x7 convenient store round the corner
3. Great music
4. Greater lungpower
5. Fabulous contacts in the Dilli Police
6. Two people capable of furnishing surety bonds of three lakh rupees, each
7. The will to sacrifice the first half of the next day

I have a friend who has earned the title of *Shutter*. Mr. Shutter starts contacting planet earth only when most people are getting ready for bed. Once affirmative action is taken by kindred spirits, distances in Dilli become a pleasant journey. A dependable, tried-and-tested, unfailing 'insomnia buddy' who constantly lights up the darkest hours before the morning, Mr. Shutter is not only present to open another bottle but will also give you a hand to pull down the shutter of a bar.

In Dilli, 'till sunlight do us apart' groups abound. The interactions are meaningful, usually culminating in the baring of souls, among other things.

Late night flirtations on social sites have led to real dates.

Late night partying in each other's homes have created joint families.

Memorable nights have culminated in more memorable nights.

So who wants to become regular and see the insomnia buddies disappear from the radar?

59

Saanu Ki

'If you survive in this city, you can survive anywhere in the world.' Even the Mughals must have heard that one.

In Dilli, tip-toe around the social minefield to avoid getting blown up to pieces because the toes you step on today might turn up a metre and half below the ass you may have to kiss tomorrow.

So be artfully evasive. Your popularity shall be based on a total lack of principles and values, the willing desertion of your dear ones at their hour of need, and your single-minded focus on being perceived as the neutral party. When your friend gets into a fight, don't take sides. When the axe hangs over someone's head, look the other way.

Be a righteous junky, a weapon of social destruction, always commenting on others without them getting a whiff of it. Play on another's weakness, confuse the entire world, create the impression of universal love. Initiate a rumour, ostracise an unsuspecting being. Defame, degrade. Dig dirt and splash it around, then offer a compassionate shoulder. Hold out the box of tissues, pat the back, prepare a warm beverage, advice the victim to not give two hoots about what is being said (even if you got those Chinese whispers going) with an innocuous *'Saanu ki?'*—a popular Punjabi expression (literal translation 'What is it to me/ us?'; literary translation 'How are we concerned?') Fruitful exercise. Try it.

Over dinner at a friend's house, I was introduced to a nice and charming couple. Preened the hostess, 'Oh you know, he is such a great blah, blah, blah and she is really a wonderful blah, blah, blah. You have to see their new farmhouse. It is one of the best blah, blah.' That lasted for a fair part of the evening…till the couple left for another 'friend's party.' Everyone present, barring me, heaved a sigh of relief and chorused, 'What a miser the husband is and that wife is such an upstart.' Before I could adjust the angle and distance of my eyebrows from my eyelids, I was made privy to unflattering stories about them, some going back decades. Bets were placed on whether they would offer to pay a bill anytime this century and so on.

After picking on them for over an hour, the conversation concluded with a *'Saanu ki'* and all was back to normal.

Moral of the story: hear evil, talk evil, do evil. Then wipe the slate clean by uttering those two magic words *'Saanu ki.'*

60

This is the End, My Friend

Yes, that era has gone by. Glorious, golden days (and nights) of the '90s, spent at Ghungroo, Oasis, My Kind of Place, Djinn. Life came with style in the form of cigar-pumping, weapon-yielding Godfather clones with a hint of Scarface.

Just a handful of luxury cars burnt rubber on Dilli's road. Every server knew them and their drinks. Their names were enshrined in all the four bars; their presence a humbling experience for the managers who said grace with every order they placed.

Today they refer to themselves as old money to distinguish themselves from the cheap thrills of new money, even if the old money has long returned to dust. Like dispossessed maharajas, they repeat stories of glorious conquests as you fight to keep a yawn at bay.

~

Time wrings out the old and rings in the new. One day, we must mull over the youthful T-shirts, animal-print jumpsuits and Barbie hairstyle with bangs; mug shots from 1991; bandaged feet before and after a night in heels; the spandex sheath that cuts off oxygen supply to the lungs while we reach out for those inhalers...

To hold on to the slipping sand, consider Social Service or a Guest Relations outfit, or recite the *mantra* below 108 times at 4:30 a.m. facing westwards for that's where the sun sets:

Twinkle Twinkle Little Star,
Put me back on the social radar.
Up above the world so high,
Way above those who still fly.
But when all the strength is gone,
There will be none to look down upon,
Then how do I tackle my plight,
As I wage a losing fight.
In the dark I shall quietly weep,
Trying to hang on to my keep.
I shall never shut an eye,
Another invite and I'll surely fly.
Till the pacemaker in my chest
Reminds me to look my graceful best,
When none shall remember who we are.
Twinkle Twinkle Little Star.